TRUTH-OR-DATE.COM

BY

NINA HARRINGTON

First published in Great Britain 2012
by Mills & Boon, an imprint of Harlequin (UK) Limited.
Large Print edition 2013
Harlequin (UK) Limited, Eton House,
18-24 Paradise Road, Richmond, Surrey TW9 1SR

© Nina Harrington 2012

ISBN: 978 0 263 23166 3

Harlequin (UK) policy is to use papers that are natural, renewable and recyclable products and made from wood grown in sustainable forests. The logging and manufacturing process conform to the legal environmental regulations of the country of origin.

Printed and bound in Great Britain
by CPI Antony Rowe, Chippenham, Wiltshire

TRUTH-OR-DATE.COM

CHAPTER ONE

From: Andromeda@ConstellationOfficeServices
To: saffie@saffronthechef
Subject: Our least favourite school friend and on-line dating
Hey Saffie.

I know, I know. I should have listened when you tried to warn me against working part-time for Elise van der Kamp in the first place.

Do you remember when Elise signed up with that expensive Internet dating agency for young executives? Well, now she has decided she is too busy to write her own emails and that I should do it for her. Write a few emails, she said. Then a few more. Just to get the ball rolling. After all, what else are personal assistants for?

Right.

I almost told her what to do with her job, but then she offered me a special bonus, which should be enough to pay for that professional illustrator's course I've been yearning to go on. It would be perfect. And just what I need to be taken seriously as an artist.

Not much has changed from school, has it? Elise knew I couldn't turn it down.

So guess who has been wooing potential Christmas party arm candy for our least favourite school friend every evening for the past week? Oh, yes.

Well, things have just sunk to a new low.

Ten minutes ago she texted me to say that she has to dash off to Brazil on some urgent business and—wait for it—she has changed her mind about the whole online dating thing. Apparently it is far too sordid and risky and she doesn't want her reputation sullied by that kind of thing.

Sullied! Can you believe it? I don't think she even read one of the emails I sent or the lovely replies I got back from the boys who had rearranged their schedules to meet her for coffee this week.

The real problem is that the first coffee date is tonight. As in half an hour from now, and it is far too late to cancel. This one's username is #sportybloke and he sounds really nice over the Internet. I can't stand the idea of the poor man sitting there all alone waiting for #citygirl Elise to show. I know what it's like to be stood up and I wouldn't wish that on anyone. And I do feel sort of responsible.

Do you think I should go and meet him? And explain?

Ahhrrggg.

Hope that slave-driver of a master chef isn't working you too hard in Paris.

Wish me luck. Andy

From: saffie@saffronthechef
To: Andromeda@ConstellationOfficeServices
Andy Davies, you are making my head spin. I cannot believe that you would agree to go onto an Internet dating site posing as Elise van der Kamp. I mean…Elise? Social skills of a piranha and twice as mean? Sheesh.

I am not in the least surprised that she chose a friendly person to write her emails for her.

As for the coffee date? I think you would feel better if you took a minute to go there and apologise in person. But be careful. Executive type? Being stood up and lied to? He could get cross.

Use your charm. And take extra sharp pencils. Just in case.

Love ya. Saffie the kitchen slave

ANDROMEDA Davies stepped down from the red London bus and darted under the shelter of the nearest shop doorway. The November rain pounded on the fabric awning above her head and bounced off the pavement of the narrow street in this smart part of the city.

Her gaze skipped between the pedestrians scurrying for cover until it settled on the giant mocha-cup bistro sign directly across the street.

Light from within the coffee shop streamed out in vertical bands like strobe lights between the pedestrians onto the wet pavement. She had already been here twice that week on a mission to find the perfect location for a first Internet date for Elise. It was ideal. Central, well lit, spacious and very public. They served hot food and the coffee was pretty good too.

Taking a deep breath, Andy tugged her shoulder bag across her chest, and hit the button on the handle of her umbrella with her thumb. It was so typical that the only umbrella she possessed was purple with pink cartoon flowers on the top and had been a gift from when she'd worked as a temp at a company that made novelty items for children's parties.

In her current financial state she was hardly one to complain and if it kept her dry that would be a bonus—but Elise would have taken one look at it and thrown it in the bin.

Her cover story was that it was a unique design from an up-and-coming fashion designer who specialised in one-off graphics. Nobody else would have an umbrella just like it and…

Lies, lies, lies, lies. All lies. Some little fluffy cloud white lies and some great big stonking massive thundercloud of lies. But lies just the same.

Andy closed her eyes and wallowed in ten seconds of self-pity and shame before shaking herself out of it.

This had been her decision. Nobody had forced her to agree to impersonate Elise van der Kamp on the dating site. She could have refused and insisted that Elise write her own correspondence with these busy city boys. But Elise knew that she wouldn't turn it down. Not when she was waving a sweet cash bonus as bait to lure her in.

Andy dropped her shoulders, and shoved her free hand into the pocket of her trendy dark navy raincoat with white piping, which she had snatched up from a charity shop in an exclusive part of town.

The things she did for her art!

She really didn't have to worry about her umbrella or how she looked as long as she kept to her plan. All she had to do was dash in, wait for #sportybloke to arrive, apologise politely on behalf of Elise and then leave. The whole thing would be over in ten minutes.

Of course the girl he was expecting was the efficient and sophisticated executive director of one of the largest corporate promotion companies in Britain. Or, as Elise had insisted that she add to her online dating profile, aspiring marketing guru to the world.

Gag.

Ten minutes. And then she could get back on the bus and switch to being plain old Andy Davies, part-time personal assistant to Elise during the day, mostly unpaid illustrator in the evenings and weekend art historian, aspiring to pay the bills.

She would not be here at all if Elise had not suggested that she could 'take care' of the first round of emails—'so that she was not wasting her time on the no-hopers'.

Charming. And some of the men sounded lovely. *On their profiles.*

'I know I can rely on you completely to manage my social diary,' Elise had said with her full-beam smile. 'There is simply no one else I could trust with my personal information. But we have been friends for so long, Andromeda. I just know that you will be totally discreet. Wonderful!'

Um. *Right.* It had probably never even crossed Elise's mind that Andy had to juggle her hours at the last minute to fit all of the work in. But she had done it—just. Maybe now that Elise had pulled the plug on the Internet dating, they could both go back to what passed for a normal life in her crazy world. Like planning the Christmas and New Year party circuit.

Providing, of course, she survived explaining to #sportybloke that #citygirl had no intention of turning up to meet him.

Now that did give her the shivers. That and the rivulet of rain water spilling out from the awning.

Exhaling slowly, Andy glanced from side to side to find a gap in the stream of people who had their heads down, their umbrellas braced forward against the driving rain and oblivious to anyone who might walk in their way.

Seizing on a momentary lull, Andy lifted her umbrella high and dashed out onto the road in the stationary rush hour traffic. She had almost made it, when she had to dive sideways to dodge a bicycle courier and planted her right foot into a deep puddle. Dirty cold water splashed up into her smart high-heeled ankle boots and trickled down inside, making her gasp with shock.

Hissing under her breath, Andy stepped up onto the kerb, closed her umbrella, which had totally failed to keep her dry, and opened the door to the coffee shop and stepped inside.

Water dripping from every part of her, Andy shook the rain from her hair and inhaled the glorious deep, rich aroma of the freshly ground coffee beans. She was looking forward to the day when she could afford real coffee at home to replace the cheapest supermarket-brand instant coffee. The aroma combined with the background noise of the coffee shop—a low steady hum of voices, coffee grinders and espresso machines—created a wonderful soundtrack that she had every intention of enjoying, seeing as Elise was picking up the bill.

Andy gazed around the terracotta and cream walls to the groups of people sitting on the pale oak chairs behind red-and-white gingham check tablecloths.

No sign of the Hawaiian shirt #sportybloke had said that he was going to wear—and she was not likely to miss that type of clothing on a cold wet evening in early November in the centre of London.

Andy moved to the counter, bought her Americano coffee and took a seat at the small square table in the corner with her back to the wall. She propped her pink-and-purple umbrella against the wall, slipped off her raincoat over the back of the chair and ran her hands down the skirt of her favourite grey business suit.

A flutter of nervous apprehension winged across her stomach.

This was so ridiculous.

She wasn't here on a real date. There was no need to be nervous.

She was here to apologise for Elise. That was all.

So what if she had tried to imagine what #sportybloke would look like in person? You could only tell so much from an online thumbnail photograph, and they could certainly be deceptive.

It was only natural to be curious, wasn't it? Especially when #sportybloke told stories about the social life of a surfer in exotic places like Hawaii and California that had made her laugh out loud. He had a sense of humour…and he would certainly need one if he was dating Elise.

Andy bit down on her lower lip. Maybe coming here was not such a good idea. What if he was a total disappointment? And Saffie had a point. He had every right to be annoyed with her—and Elise—for tricking him. But she had to put it right with #sportybloke, tell him the truth face to face and apologise in person. She owed it to him— and herself.

Andy looked around the coffee shop at all of the happy couples, laughing and chatting merrily away over their lattes and pastries, and her heart twanged a little. But she sniffed and shook it off.

She wasn't looking for a date. Far from it—this was her time to do her own thing without having to worry about rushing back to the office where she had worked with her so-called ex-boyfriend, Nigel, to sort out his project for him. She had learnt her lesson. No more lies. No more half-truths and self-delusion. In fact, no more boyfriends at all, if her last one was anything to go by. She was quite happy on her own. *Thank you!*

Andy checked her wristwatch. Ten minutes. Then she would finally be able to steal back the few spare hours she had in the day to work on the type of paperwork she loved most.

Hiding a quick smirk, Andy dived into her large shoulder bag and pulled out her sketch pad and pencil. The museum she worked at part-time had agreed to see her five favourite hand-crafted Christmas card designs with the view to possibly selling them in their shop and she was so close to being finished! This was her chance to persuade the museum to showcase her calligraphy and artwork.

Andy was so engrossed in a sketch of a decorative

scroll of strawberries and clover leaves that it took a blast of cold damp air from the open door to snap her back into the present moment. She shivered in her thin suit and looked up in surprise.

A towering dark-haired man filled the space where the entrance had been, before he closed the door behind him.

His tanned face was glowing from the rain and wind and he ran the fingers of his right hand back through his long damp hair from forehead to neck in a single natural motion.

The water droplets stood proud on the shoulders of a hip-length waterproof sailing jacket, which he was slowly unzipping as if he were a male stripper in a cabaret act. Umm. And she would be right there in the front row telling him not to rush.

Wow. He certainly had the body to pull it off should he decide on a change in direction, and as he rolled back his shoulders with a casual shrug Andy sucked in a breath in anticipation, and then exhaled very slowly.

Yup. *Hawaiian shirt.*

His square jaw was so taut it might have been sculpted. But it was his mouth that knocked the air out of her lungs, and had her clinging onto the edge of the table for support.

Plump lips smiled wide above his lightly stubbled chin, so that the bow was sharp between the smile lines. It was a mouth made for smiling, with slight dimples either side.

The short-haired #sportybloke who had posed for the corporate shot on the online profile had been wearing a suit and tie and looked like a clone of all the other business execs. But the man in the flesh was something else. For once the photo had not done him justice. At all.

His button-fly denims sat low on his slim hips but there was no mistaking that he was pure muscle beneath those tight pants. Because as he stood there for a second, his hands thrust deep into his trouser pockets, looking from table to table, scanning the horizon that was the confines of the coffee shop, every movement he made seemed magnified and as glaringly in your face as the scarlet-and-blue tropical flowers on his shirt.

The entire room seemed to shrink around him.

How did he do that? How did he just waltz in and master the room as though he were in command of the space and everyone in it?

This man was outdoors taken to the next level. No wonder he worked for a company making sports clothing. She could certainly imagine him standing at the helm of some racing yacht, head high, legs braced. The master of all he surveyed.

The hair on the back of her neck prickled with recognition. Her father had been like that once, when he worked in the city. So confident in his right to be the self-proclaimed master of the universe that when the financial crash came his world, his sanity and his identity tumbled down with it.

It was a pity that she was on a boyfriend ban. Because #sportybloke was truly the best-looking man she had seen in a very long time.

And then he saw her, but instead of giving her the up-and-down, toes-to-hair 'beauty pageant' special once-over, his gaze locked onto her face and stayed there, unmoving for a few seconds, before the corner of his mouth slid into a lazy smile.

The corners of those amazing eyes crinkled slightly and the warmth of that smile seemed to heat the air between them. And at that moment, this smile was for her. And her heart leapt. More than a little. But just enough to recognise that the blush of heat racing through her neck and face were not only due to the piping-hot coffee she had barely sipped.

In that instant Andy knew what it felt like to be the most important and most beautiful person in the room, but instead of squirming and wanting to slide under the table she lifted her chin. Heart thumping. Brain spinning. An odd and unfamiliar tension hummed down her veins. Every cell of her suddenly alive and tuned into the vibrations emanating from his body.

Suddenly she wanted to preen and flick her hair and roll her shoulders back so that she could stick her chest out.

It was as if she had been dusted with instant lust powder.

Wow.

#sportybloke had truly arrived.

Sitting up a little straighter on her chair, Andy quickly swept away her sketch pad and focused her gaze on the arrangement of the menus on the table, trying to find something to do with her hands, only too aware that he was still watching her.

She could practically feel the heat of that laser-beam gaze burning a hole through her forehead and was surprised that there was no smell of smoke or a scorch mark on the wall behind her.

Even though she had chosen the most spacious coffee shop she could find, this man weaving his way towards her seemed to block the light. According to his profile he was six feet two inches but he certainly filled every inch. He was tall and tanned and broad-shouldered and muscular and every ounce of his attention was totally focused on her.

His feet slowed as he reached her table and she looked up into a pair of eyes the colour of dark bitter chocolate below heavy dark eyebrows and wavy brown hair. He had eyes a girl could drown in and not want to come up for air. And they locked onto hers as though they could see into her soul, wander around for a while, looking for trouble, then move on leaving her lonely and bereft.

'I'm a sort of a sportybloke. You may be expecting me, city girl.'

His transatlantic voice was rich, deep and came from low down in his diaphragm, giving it a certain roughness that resonated inside her head.

It was the kind of voice that should be on the radio promoting late-night ballads, but it had no place at all in a small London coffee shop where she was in touching distance of its owner.

He just stood there, patiently waiting for her reply, with a smile on his lips and a body aimed at her. A male cover model made flesh.

Just hearing his voice made her glad that she was sitting down and, judging by the glances from the other women on the nearby tables, allure this powerful had a range of at least ten feet.

What was he doing here? On an Internet date of all things? This man could win a gold medal in charming women without even trying hard!

'Absolutely,' she lied, horrified at how pathetic and squeaky her voice sounded, and she tugged at the lilac silk scarf Elise had chosen as her marker. 'Scarf and all.'

'I am sorry I'm late.' He smiled, shrugging off his waterproof and throwing it casually onto the wooden floor behind her chair, showering the planks and smothering her umbrella in the process. 'Had to take someone to the airport and the traffic was pretty bad. Thanks for waiting.'

'No problem,' she replied, and held out her hand. 'It's nice to finally meet you in person.'

He stepped forward and grasped hold of her hand and his long fingers wrapped around hers with a strong, masterful grip, which was probably perfect for grappling ropes on sailboats and back-slapping athletes, but left her fingers feeling as though she had been sitting on them for several minutes. But who needed blood anyway?

Inappropriate and totally crazy thoughts about the effect those same fingers could have on other parts of her body flitted through Andy's mind and it was a relief when he broke contact first and slid down into the smallish wooden chair opposite, which seemed far too flimsy for his body.

'You too. Corporate promotions. Tricky stuff.'

Andy felt her heart rate increase several notches as he moved even closer.

Keep to the script. Keep to the script. Give him five minutes to get a coffee, and then break it to him gently. Talk business. That usually works.

She took a long drink of coffee to give her brain a chance to catch up and form something close to a sensible reply. 'It can be. But I suspect that every successful entrepreneur has to take risks. Even in sportswear.'

His brown eyes focused on her face, but there was just enough of a crunch between the dark brows to capture her attention. 'Damn right.'

Then one side of his mouth lifted into a half-smile. 'You could almost say that was the best part. Pushing yourself against the limits, knowing just what kind of risk you are taking. Yeah. I guess that we are both in the risk business. Can I get you another coffee?'

And without waiting for her reply he lifted his head and, like a genie from a lamp, the barista instantly appeared on their side of the counter. 'Two of what the lady had and I'll take an omelette. Three eggs, ham and mushroom. No onion, heavy on the herbs. And can you throw in some of those Panini and a couple of cookies? Cheers.'

Two fingers to the forehead and their server was gone. Amazing.

Andy looked in astonishment to the counter, where the two girls were feverishly working on the order, and then back to #sportybloke, who was sitting back, legs outstretched to one side. Watching her.

'Do you always do that?' She asked with a quick jab of her head towards the counter.

He blinked and hit her with a grin that displayed his straight white teeth to best effect. 'Do what? Order coffee? Yeah, I might do that now and again. Especially in a coffee shop.'

'I mean, do you always just shout out the order from your chair instead of going up to the counter like everyone else? And how do you know that I needed another coffee? I might have preferred a tea for a change. Or maybe even one of those hot steak sandwiches?'

His reply was to rest his bare arms on the table, hands loose and relaxed, and lean the top half of his long wide frame towards her from the hips so that she had to fight the urge to lean back against the wall and protect her space.

The top two buttons of his shirt stretched open as the fabric stretched over a broad chest, and revealed a hint of deeply tanned skin, and more than a few dark chest hairs.

At this distance she could have reached out and touched the curved flicks of dark wavy hair that had fallen over one side of his temple, but she had the idea that he would like that far too much, so she simply lifted her chin and inhaled a long calming breath through her nose.

Big mistake.

Instead of a background aroma of coffee and baked goods, she was overwhelmed with the scent of gentle rain on fresh-cut grass blended with lime zest, which was tangy against the sweetness of the air.

He smelt wonderful. Fresh, distinctive and on a scale of one to ten on the testosterone level she would give it a twelve. Because there was no mistake. The man below the flamboyant floral shirt that the dreadful Nigel would have completely refused to wear, even for a bet, was certainly adding a lot of himself to the mix. From the sun-bleached hair on his arms and the way the muscles in his neck flexed when he moved, to the 'know it all' confidence in the smile he was giving her at that moment, he was off the scale.

And then he ramped it up a notch by lowering the tone of his voice so that she was the only person who would be able to hear him whisper in words that were as smooth as molten chocolate.

'I took a chance. *City girl.*'

Then he slid his arms into his lap, sat back against the wooden chair and winked at her.

CHAPTER TWO

A CHANCE? He took a chance? Oh! Could he *be* more of a caveman and testosterone driven?

And he knew it! He knew exactly what effect he was having.

And suddenly every alarm bell in her body started sounding all at once.

Why on earth did a man this gorgeous need to meet women on the Internet?

It was obvious from his emails that he was a flirt, but this man looked as though he was getting ready to beat his chest and roar or if that didn't work, sling the nearest stone club over his shoulder and head out into the rain looking for dinosaurs to slay.

His too-long dark chocolate-brown hair was tousled and so unkempt that one heady thick wave fell forward across his high cheekbone, and he flicked it back with his fingertips. It was a move that any professional fashion model would be proud to have mastered so perfectly—while still looking manly and gruff.

Then there was that mouth.

#sportybloke had an expression that was somewhere between suggestive and cheeky and as infectious as chicken pox. Andy had to fight from smiling automatically in return.

Until now she had believed that she was immune to such charms. After all, she had been exposed to this type of infection many times before and just about survived.

But this man was a carrier for a super powerful version of charm that no amount of medical science and previous experience had a chance of fighting off.

She might have guessed.

#sportybloke was one of *them*.

According to his online profile he ran a sportswear company with his brother and spent a lot of time promoting water sports overseas. Their speciality was surfing gear.

Well, from the looks of #sportybloke he was just another wealthy, arrogant and handsome entrepreneur who had been in the right place at the right time and had made his pile of money and was determined to flash it at every opportunity. A man like him spent his winters at some luxury ski resort and his summers bumming it around the Caribbean on other people's yachts while his was being built to his own specifications.

Little wonder that he probably expected everyone to jump when he clicked his fingers, when, in fact, CEOs of international sports companies had all the time and money in the world.

Sheesh. Well, Andy had news for #sportybloke. The dinosaur was right here in the room and she was looking at him. Okay, so that was no hardship, but it was definitely time to get back to the script and earn that bonus that she knew Elise would pay, even if she had pulled the plug on the whole Internet dating business.

Just tell him and get it over with. He can cope!

Andy took a breath for courage, her back braced. But just as she was about to blurt out who she was and why she was there, the food and fresh coffees arrived and she was temporarily distracted by the delicious aroma from two cheese and ham freshly grilled Panini and crisp chocolate-chunk-and-hazelnut cookies.

One of the bar staff actually whimpered slightly

under her breath as she slid the plate of steaming hot, fragrant herby omelette in front of #sportybloke, who thanked her with a smile.

Unbelievable.

'Ladies first,' he breathed and gestured towards the Panini; he had deftly cut each in half diagonally and left them in the centre of the table. They were oozing with molten cheese and tomato in between the crunchy bread and her mouth was already watering at the aroma, but just as she was about to say no her stomach growled in anticipation of the fat and carb treat that was on display.

'Thank you,' she murmured, leaning forward towards him, 'but there is something I need to tell you and it is quite urgent. You see, I'm not who you think I am. When I sent you those emails I...'

Suddenly a chair was knocked over on the next table only inches away from where Andy was sitting. An older man was on his feet, gasping in air through his nose, his hands clutched tight onto the sides of the table. He was panicking, his eyes darting from side to side. Face and neck red.

Without waiting for permission Andy darted out from her seat. 'Someone please help. He's choking.' Oblivious to the sound of people standing and shuffling chairs, she gave the man an almighty thump between his shoulder blades with the heel of her hand. Her hand ached with the effort and she was puffing slightly but her back slap had no effect.

Andy stepped back to inhale and was just about to repeat the process when #sportybloke appeared at her side, stepped into the gap, linked his hands in front of the now very wheezy and panicky diner and pulled sharply upwards with all the force that a muscular man over six feet tall with long arms could produce on a crouched person's stomach. A sizeable piece of unchewed steak sandwich shot out onto the check tablecloth and the diner sucked in breath after breath, his shoulders shaking with relief.

#sportybloke gave him a quick nod in reply to the handshake and man-thumped the stranger on the arm before stepping back to their table. Apparently oblivious to the slight cheer that had gone up from the other patrons and the anxious waitresses.

But instead of sitting down, he clamped his fingers tightly around the back of his chair and exhaled slowly from deep inside his chest, with a definite wince.

'Anything the matter?' she asked, quietly.

His gaze shot onto her face. It was fierce and intense, and for one microsecond she had an insight into the power and strength of this man who could freeze her to ice with just one glance.

But then he blinked and his eyes softened. 'Leg cramp.' He coughed and slapped his upper thigh with the flat of his hand. 'I'm not used to sitting around for long periods. But I'm fine. Thanks.'

And he immediately pushed his chair closer to the wall so that he could sit down with his right leg stretched out in front of him.

Andy slid back in the chair and sat back to wait for her heart to stop thumping before blinking, swallowing hard and pulling her chair to the table.

'Well. If you're okay. That was…different,' she said, looking over #sportybloke's shoulder. 'If I was the suspicious type I might think that you set that up just to impress me. Luckily for you I'm not, but I didn't see emergency first aid on your online dating profile. Is that new?'

'My first regular paid job was as a lifeguard in Cornwall. Compulsory first-aid training. Although

I can't say that I have used that move for a while. Glad to have helped—but you did okay for a city girl. One tip? Thump harder next time.'

'Next time? I don't want there to be a next time, thank you.'

She held out her right hand in front of her and watched the fingers tremble. 'How can you stay so cool? I'm a wreck.'

His reply was to smile and seize hold of her hand between the palms of both of his, trapping it inside as he slowly moved his hands up and down, inch by inch, massaging life and heat and stimulation into the nerves.

His skin was warm and surprisingly soft except for the callouses on the fingers and inside his palms, but there was no mistaking the hidden strength in those hands and fingers.

She liked hands, always had. It was usually one of the first things she noticed about a person. And this man had spectacular hands. Long slender fingers with clean short nails. His knuckles were scarred and bruised as though they had been bashed at regular intervals.. Sinewy. Powerful.

They were clever, fast, working hands, and for the first time Andy wondered if she had made a mistake slotting #sportybloke into the arrogant CEO slot. These were not the hands of an office worker like the men she usually met. Far from it.

Um. Maybe he had been telling the truth about his surfing line in those emails?

'Being cool has nothing to do with it. I simply knew what I had to do and did it. Feeling better now? Great. Let's eat.'

He slid his hands away and her rock-steady fingers waggled back. But to her disgust she already missed having his warm strong hand around hers.

Then he cut the omelette into quarters, then eighths before spearing a portion with some of the salad garnish and carefully closing his mouth around the fork. Then slowly, slowly, drew the fork from his mouth.

And suddenly Andy found that her neck had become amazingly hot for some reason and she put down her dinner to loosen her scarf.

He was eating an omelette using cutlery. That was all. And the whole fork thing was not sensuous at all. Oh, no. Not a bit. Well… Maybe a little.

Well, that clinched it.

This man was way too handsome to be single

and looking for girls online. And he could speak in joined-up sentences and use cutlery.

There had to be something wrong with him.

She had heard about married or engaged men who went on Internet dating sites to have extra-marital affairs with unsuspecting girls. Perhaps he already had a perfectly charming lovely lady back at home? Or he was actually a journalist doing a documentary about desperate sad girls who met men through Internet dating.

She inhaled sharply.

Focus, Andy, focus. Stop letting your imagination run away with you.

She took a breath and her words came tumbling out in one huge rush.

'I need to tell you something. I am not the #citygirl executive you were expecting. My boss is. Only she had to go away on urgent business and it was too late to cancel. So, I came instead to apologise. Sorry.'

And then she sat back, dropped her hands into her lap, focused her gaze on his chin and waited for the fireworks to start.

The man on the other side of the table continued chewing for a moment, then put down his cutlery, crossed his arms, stretched out his neck and seemed to double his size. If he was intending to be imposing and maybe a little intimidating, his plan was working perfectly.

He stared at her through slightly narrowed eyes, his eyebrows low and dark, and she had to fight down the sudden urge to start chewing at her fingernails.

'So let me get this straight. You're not the girl I was supposed to meet here tonight.'

Andy pressed her lips together and risked a small apologetic shrug.

'And you're not a company executive?'

She shook her head very rapidly from side to side.

'I see,' he replied with something close to disappointment in his voice. 'So how do I get to meet the girl who wrote those emails? Or has she got cold feet?'

She blinked twice before answering. 'Oh, that was me. I wrote the emails. My boss paid me to write them for her, you see, and I really enjoyed chatting to you and learning about your life as...'

A low growl stopped her mid tracks. 'Paid you? To write them. Right. So just who are you and what are you really doing here?' he asked, and slid the whole top half of his body across the table towards her.

She tried shuffling backwards as he invaded what little personal space she had left but it was no use. Unless she wanted to leap sideways like a gazelle and make a run for it she was stuck. It was confession time. If he let her get a word in edgeways.

'Is this some sort of game you and your boss play with men you set up on the Internet? For all I know you could be pretending to be your PA because you don't like what you see or maybe you're using your boss's Internet account to meet someone above your pay scale. Am I close? Which one is it?'

Andy stared at him in horror, the blood pounding in her neck.

'A game? Of course it isn't a game. Elise doesn't even know that I'm here. And I would never use her account to meet people. That's a terrible accusation. No, it's nothing like that. Nothing at all.'

'Okay. Then what is this all about? Why are you here?'

'Well, I am beginning to wonder, because, if you

must know, my boss cancelled less than an hour ago and I didn't like the thought of you sitting here all alone waiting for a date who has stood you up. There. That's it. Happy now?'

And before he had a chance to answer, Andy picked up the Panini with both hands and took a huge bite. And the second her teeth hit the toasted bread, a large squeeze of tomato shot out and hit her straight on the chest. And her white blouse. Her only, her favourite, her best and most expensive, white blouse.

Gulping down the rest of her overfull mouthful of food, she tried to scrub at the spot with her napkin. Only it was pink and made out of paper so that she now had a pink dye and a hot tomato stain on her blouse.

She put down her shredded napkin, took a quick glance at #sportybloke, who was looking at her in disbelief.

'Fast food. Always a risky business. The steak sandwich is not the only dangerous item on the menu,' she murmured, sighed out loud, picked up the Panini and took another bite. She couldn't do any more damage so she might as well finish her food.

#sportybloke blinked several times, pushed his shoulders hard back against the chair and unfolded his arms so he could stretch them out on the table, his palms flat on the gingham. The white scars on the backs of his hands and knuckles were just large enough for her to notice, but then she had to look at something, because he was doing the laser stare again.

His gaze seemed to be locked onto her face, as though he was looking for something, and she tried desperately not to squirm. And failed.

'Happy would be pushing it, but I completely agree.' He nodded, a strange smirk on his face, then tapped his forefinger against his full pink lower lip, then pointed towards her. 'About the food. Especially the cheese.'

Cheese? What cheese?

Andy patted her napkin against her lip in a dainty and ladylike fashion and all was going well until she dropped it back to her lap to reveal a string of molten yellow plastic-looking cheese, which must have been dangling from the corner of her mouth.

Well. So much for the sophisticated and elegant look.

'That's better,' he said with a fixed smile, sitting back. 'And the name is Miles, by the way. Now where were we? Oh, yes. Being stood up. Does that still happen?'

Miles? She looked at him with raised eyebrows.

She had rain-damp hair, a stained blouse and she had been sitting there in blissful ignorance of the fact that cheese strings were dangling from her lips.

Why did he trust her with his real name? If it was his real name.

Her mouth opened, ready to share her name, but then she closed it again. *Not yet. But she could answer his question.*

She paused and looked up at the ceiling. 'Oh, yes, it has happened to me more than once. I think that's why I hated the idea of doing it to someone else. Yes, I know that we have only talked through emails, but texting is not the same as apologising in person. Or at least it isn't to me. That probably makes me sound very old-fashioned, but that's the way I am.'

He seemed to think about that for a second before replying. 'I happen to agree. And your boss doesn't know that you are here?'

Andy shook her head. 'She's changed her mind about the whole Internet dating business. But there wasn't enough time to call you and cancel. So here I am.'

Then she braved a smile over the top of her sandwich. 'I hope you're not too annoyed or disappointed. Especially since I've eaten most of your food and I'm not actually your proper date.'

He sat back, eyebrows high, and pressed one hand to his chest. 'My pleasure. You have seen through my evil plan to win over a lady with toasted cheese and coffee. I feel the shame.'

'You should.' Andy nodded and inspected the last part of her Panini. 'Even though this was a most superior cheesy snack. So thank you for that.'

'Glad you approve,' he murmured, and raised his coffee beaker. 'Here's to cheesy snacks, although I am curious about something. Does your boss often ask you to pimp for her?'

Only just as the words left his mouth Andy was swallowing some coffee and between spluttering and coughing it took her a while before she could attempt to reply with a raspy voice. 'First time. And the last. We went to school together so I suppose Elise trusted me not to let her down.' She flashed him a glance. 'Did I? Let her down?'

A long, slow, languorous smile crept like dawn across the whole of his face, and then he wrapped his hands around his beaker. 'I might have chatted to a couple of girls. But this is the first Internet date I have ever agreed to.'

He rested his elbows on the table to support his chin. 'The only one. Does that answer your question?'

Andy froze, her coffee beaker suspended in mid-air.

'This is your first Internet date?'

'Absolutely. So far, not quite what I expected, but getting better by the minute.'

Her hand dropped. 'Oh.'

Of course it is—fool. He doesn't need to go on the Internet to meet women. But it did make her wonder. *Why? Why now?*

'I enjoyed reading about all the wonderful countries you have visited for your work.' She twirled one hand towards his shirt. 'I suppose that must be a problem for your, um…romantic relationships.'

Oh, shut up now before you make an even

greater fool of yourself, you idiot. Andy winced and picked at some salad, to avoid looking at him.

'My romantic relationships?' He sniffed. 'Actually my romantic relationships, as you call them, are just fine. That isn't the problem. Just the opposite if anything—I spend my days surrounded by sporty girls of all shapes and sizes, and usually they are wearing remarkably little in the way of clothing.'

He lifted his chin and smiled. 'Did I mention that we specialise in water sports? Everything from paddle boarding to kite surfing. Our bikinis are very popular.'

A short chuckle and a nasal snort made her blink. 'No, I have plenty of female company. But I don't get to meet other kinds of women. And now I'm back in London, it might be interesting to meet girls who know more about the city than surfboards and sunblock. Plus I happen to enjoy meeting new people and getting to know them.'

She leant forwards, glancing from side to side as though about to tell him a secret of some sort.

'I have a terrible fault.'

His eyebrows rose towards the ceiling but he did not take the bait.

'Curiosity.' Andy nodded. 'I am well known for

it. So you see, I can't help but wonder…why now? What made you decide to come out on a wet night to meet this particular girl when you don't even know her name?'

And without permission or any kind of warning, he clasped his long fingers around the palm of her right hand, raised it to his mouth and kissed her knuckles for two seconds before releasing her hand.

'I wanted to meet the girl who wrote those emails. The girl I am looking at right now.'

His lips had been warm and full and soft and she was so totally taken back by how gentle and tender that ultra-soft whisper of his lips on her skin had been that she just sat there, still, and in silence. While he smiled at her. And this time his eyes were smiling as well as his mouth and all she could hear was the sound of his breathing, slow and deep, which matched hers perfectly, breath for breath.

The coffee shop and the background clatter of people and machine and chairs being dragged on wooden floors faded into some other world which she no longer had any part in.

The air in the space between them seemed

to bristle with electricity, tense and thick with unspoken words and silences. The pulse at the side of his neck was mesmerising, strong and steady in tune with his breathing.

Killer. Absolute killer.

Then he leant slightly forwards and said in a low whisper, 'I have a confession too. My brother Jason was the one who set up my profile and filled in the forms. Apparently he got fed up of my constant complaints about not being able to find a date for when I am in London.'

He raised his coffee cup and looked at her over the top of it—but his gaze was locked onto hers and somehow it was impossible for her to look away. 'To online dating virgins everywhere,' he whispered and took a long sip of coffee. 'Perhaps we should exchange notes?'

Ah...so that was it. She should have worked it out. Miles was a sailor with a girl in every port. Online dating virgin indeed!

They looked across at one another in silence, his mouth curled into a smile for so long that the air crackled across the table.

Andy felt as though a small thermonuclear device had just been planted somewhere low in her stomach and was threatening to emerge as a girly giggle.

She did not do giggling, simpering or anything that came close. Not even for hunky hotties like the one sitting opposite her nonchalantly drinking his coffee as his gaze stared into hers, waiting to see how she responded. Maybe this was some sort of test?

'I'll drink to that,' she replied, with a smirk. 'Although it does make me wonder.'

'Wonder?'

'What were you planning to do with the hazelnut cookies?' she replied in a flash, and pressed both of her lips tight together before sitting back in her chair, her head tilted to one side.

He roared with laughter. A real laugh, head back, shoulders shaking, holding onto the flimsy table, making it rock as his whole body joined in the joke, and this time she could not help herself. And for the first time in a very long while, Andy Davies laughed. Really laughed. Laughed until the tears were running down her cheeks and she was starting to wheeze.

She never laughed like this. Ever. And it was wonderful.

Even if people on the other tables had started to give them furtive glances.

Oh, Nigel would have been *so* mortified if she had made this kind of a scene on the few times when he was with her.

Nigel. Andy felt as if a bucket of icy water had been thrown over her head, and she instantly sat up straighter in her chair and tried to clear her head.

Stupid girl. She was not here to flirt and laugh with Miles. No matter how much he had brightened up her cold, wet evening. She was not ready to flirt and laugh with anyone.

She glanced up into his smiling face and a small shiver of disappointment and regret fluttered across her shoulders.

This was a horrible mistake.

It should be Elise sitting here, not her.

But he was worth meeting. If anything he was more open and extrovert than his emails had suggested. She couldn't lie.

Andy's gaze slid over to his long, muscular, tanned arms and she inhaled slowly.

Men like Miles stood at the helm of sailing ships and jumped off mountain peaks with only a pair of skis strapped to their legs. They did not do executive buffet lunches with mini canapés and fizzy pink water, which Elise specialised in.

It was time to call a halt to this embarrassing charade and make a quick getaway.

Stealing a secret smile, Andy was just about to make her excuses and leave when her view was blocked by the long cream designer raincoat of the most notorious gossip in Nigel's office, who was standing right in front of her.

Leering.

Andy reared back in horror, a fixed smile cemented onto her face. She had walked out of Nigel's office in tears six weeks ago and this was the first time that she had met any of the people she used to work with.

Worse. There were two of them. The second most feared, time-wasting gossip in the whole office building was glaring at Miles, her mouth hanging open in shock and lust.

'Hello, Andy,' the gossip whined, her eyes flicking from Andy to Miles and then back to Andy again. 'Fancy seeing you here. I heard that you were working nights somewhere.'

'Oh. Just taking an evening off,' Andy replied,

in a casual voice, refusing to get involved in any kind of conversation with these two. 'You?'

'Thought we would catch a movie,' came the casual reply. Then her lips twisted into a knowing smirk. 'Amazing who you meet on the way.'

'Isn't it? Have a good time at the movie. See you around,' Andy replied with a quick wave of her hand, then her fingers clamped around her coffee beaker instead of the girl's neck.

Sniffing at being so obviously dismissed without being introduced to Andy's mysterious date, the two shuffled over to the only spare table, which thankfully meant that they were facing away from Andy, but from the sly sniggering glances they were giving her it was obvious that their lives were now complete.

Who needed a movie when they had just found out that Andy Davies was out with a hunky bloke in a coffee shop? Just think! Who would have thought she had the nerve, after Nigel had made such a fool of her?

It would be around the office in five minutes. In fact, they were probably texting all of their *pals* and her colleagues on their mobile phones at that very minute.

'Friends of yours?' a male voice asked from across the table.

She opened her eyes and blinked. Not only was Miles still there, but he was smiling at her and had started work picking out the whole hazelnuts from his cookie. She had been so absorbed in her own dilemma that she had forgotten about him.

'Girls I used to work with in my last job. And no, they certainly are not my friends. Far from it. I despise them.'

Now why had she said that? It wasn't their fault that she had fallen for all of the lies Nigel had told her so that she would work on his business proposals for nothing, night after night, while all the time he was living with the boss's daughter and taking the credit for her work. And she was the only one who was not in on the joke. The rest of the office had been laughing behind her back for weeks. Just waiting for Nigel to dump her the second he got his promotion. And he had. Oh, yes. And in public. And in style.

That familiar cold dark blanket of humiliation and bitter disappointment wrapped itself around Andy's shoulders, and she shivered inside her thin suit jacket.

'I see. They tell me that girls can be hard to work with. I'm sorry if my being here is going to cause you a problem back in the office.'

'Problem?' She whimpered and slumped down. 'You don't know the half of it.' Then she caught his change in breathing, and saw a flash of concern in his eyes. Tossing her head, she ran her fingers through her hair and smiled. 'Sorry. It's fine. Let's try and ignore them. They have nothing to do with my life now.'

He rested both elbows on the table and leaned forwards until his fingers were almost touching hers, and nobody else could hear what he was saying, his back to the room. 'None of my business but in my mind there are two ways to deal with office gossips. You say so what, and shrug it off. Or...' He picked up Andy's hand and started playing with it.

'What are you doing?' Andy snapped, trying to pull her hand away, but he was holding it in a vicelike grip. 'They're looking this way and taking photos on their cell phones,' she groaned in a strangled voice, as if things could get any worse.

'Excellent,' he replied, in a low calm voice. 'So

let's try the other option, and give them something to really talk about.'

There was something in his voice that should have warned her that actually things were going to suddenly get a lot worse, but her gaze was locked on his mouth as he licked his lower lip with the tip of his tongue.

Then without warning his entire body moved in one single continuous motion, so that as he lifted slightly from his chair his right hand reached back and cradled the base of her head.

And then he kissed her.

Not just a peck on the cheek. Oh, no. His warm, full, moist lips moved gently across hers in a kiss so tender and so loving that her eyes instantly filled with tears and she had to blink them away as she closed her eyes and tilted her head so that he could kiss her again.

Only this time it was deeper and she felt just the slightest tingle of his tongue, chocolate and coffee on hers before he slid his mouth away, leaving her staggered, wobbly and unable to speak and attempting to breathe again.

Wow.

Andy opened her eyes and he was breathing as

hard as she was. She could not resist staring at his full mouth, which was still wet from her kiss, and in another place and another universe she would have liked to know what it would feel like to lift that shirt over his head and find out what kind of man was able to kiss a perfect stranger like that.

She wasn't sure if she was meant to push him away and hit him for taking advantage, or pull him closer, and jump into his lap.

He did it for her. 'Andy?'

'Yes?'

'Do you think that is enough to keep the gossips happy?' he asked in a hoarse, breathless whisper.

'Oh, yes. That would do it,' Andy answered, and looked over to the girls who seemed to be huddled together over their phones. 'That will definitely do it.'

She pulled back, scraping her chair along the floor, grabbed her bag and stood up. 'Back in a moment. Too much caffeine,' she lied and almost ran to the ladies' room.

'I'll be right here,' he murmured behind her back. She turned back to look at him, as his fingers started flicking across the screen of his smart phone. The way his fingertips pressed the keys told her a lot more about his finesse and gentle touch than any online profile could.

Miles would be amazing in bed. She sighed as she turned away.

And it was only when she got inside the stall and had locked the door firmly behind her that her brain caught up with her hormones.

Miles had just called her Andy. And now he knew her real name!

She sat down, fully clothed, her elbows resting on her knees, chewing at her raggedy small fingernail, trying to come up with a cunning plan as to how to:

#Thank Miles for his understanding about Elise and pray that he had enough cash for the bill. Then thank him for the nice kiss. No—make that a very nice kiss.

#Sneak out of the coffee shop alone past the two gossips. Or maybe she should stride past with her head high? Nigel the suit was nothing compared to the gorgeousness of the man she had just left at the table.

#Come clean to Saffie. It had to be done. Elise's online coffee date had kissed her within an hour of walking through the door. Which either made her extremely lucky or a total strumpet. And she did not do strumpet. Never had. Not even when she was at school. The boys from their rival high school did not call her frosty knickers without good reason.

#Try and ignore the fact that Miles was the most attractive man that she had met in a very long time and that she would be reliving every moment of the last hour for a long time to come.

She keyed in the list on her organiser, looked at it, then shut the gizmo down and stuffed it into her bag, ripped off a long strip of toilet tissue and blew her nose loudly.

One thing was for sure. She was not going to get anything done sitting here feeling sorry for herself. Time to get going.

Andy pushed herself to her wobbly legs, turned the door handle and hobbled over to the washbasins in her high-heeled boots to try and repair the damage before facing Miles again.

She took one look at the medium-height, medium-pretty woman with the medium-brown scraggy hair in the mirror and winced.

Why had she stayed long enough to let Miles kiss her?

Miles was a flirt. A professional, Greek-god-handsome, used-to-women-falling-at-his-feet flirt. He had higher qualifications in manly allure and an honorary degree from the university of flirting and female dazzling.

And she was not in a place where she could handle that. Any of it.

He was everything she'd thought he might be from his emails. And more.

She simply wasn't up to flirting with a man like Miles and the truth was…she didn't know whether she ever would be. Time to go home.

CHAPTER THREE

MILES watched Andy stroll away from him to the other side of the room.

So what if he was a leg man?

Those cute little ankle boots showed off her shapely legs to perfection, and not even that shapeless grey business suit could hide the fact that Andy had a body that would look amazing in a swimsuit.

What was the Andy short for? Andrea? Maybe he would have a chance to find out.

If she let him.

Miles chortled to himself as he finished his coffee. It wasn't often that the old Gibson charm let him down, and he had a sneaking suspicion that there might be a back door to this coffee shop and Andy had made a run for it.

And he could hardly blame her. He had felt like doing exactly the same thing after the little announcement she had made earlier.

The whole idea that he had been set up was the one thing guaranteed to flick his switches. When she told him that she was a replacement for her boss, his first reaction was to walk out and not look back.

Which was only natural after what happened with Lori.

But that was before he realised that Andy was the girl who had written the emails that had made all of those trips to the physio almost tolerable over the past week.

Well. Jason had warned him that this #citygirl might not be the date he was expecting—and he had got that right.

She was a whole lot more.

It took guts to come here and apologise in person. Guts and a heart that did not want him to sit here on his own waiting for his date to show up. Maybe that was what he had seen in those emails? That Andy cared about people. People other than herself.

One thing was sure.

He had trusted his gut reaction every day of his sporting life, and right now it was telling him that Andy was telling him the truth. This was no trick—she had not even bothered to look the same as the girl whose blurry photo was attached to the online dating profile.

Of course he could be wrong. Lori had proved that. But there was even more to this girl Andy than he had expected. She was curious about him—and he was just as curious about her. Why on earth did she agree to write emails for her boss? This girl had a story to tell and he wouldn't mind hearing it.

At the very least she could provide the kind of distraction he would need to get through the sports event a week on Saturday.

He peered around in the direction of the ladies' room. She had taken off pretty quickly after he had kissed her. Maybe that had been a mistake? She hadn't stopped him but unless he had read the signals wrong she hadn't been expecting it, either.

Maybe she was hiding and afraid to come out in case he was actually a sex fiend who lured nice girls into coffee shops. Then kissed them in front of their least favourite workmates.

Jason was going to be furious.

Miles scanned his emails and opened the latest from Jason with a link to an article from a London magazine giving a list of the Brainiest Millionaire Bachelors in London.

And there he was—Jason Gibson of Cory Sports. His identical twin brother.

The photographer must have come to their London office because Jason was in full city-boy mode. He was wearing his trademark long-sleeved black shirt with the diamond cufflinks in the shape of a surfboard and black formal trousers. Something must have amused Jason because he had broken into a half-smile as he looked into the camera.

Miles shook his head. Even though they were so totally different in so many ways, there was no denying the fact that there had been a time when their own parents could not tell them apart.

Of course that had been before he filled out and Jason stayed boy slender.

When he thought about all of the times they had swopped places and fooled people over the years. Playing tricks on teachers and girls was their favourite—Jason was naturally more academic and a whizz at exams. He could never understand why Miles only wanted to learn about the things that interested him—like sports science and geology and the weather.

Then there had been that one time when Miles had taken the boat out to show off to some girl and it had run out of diesel in the middle of nowhere. And Jason had taken the initiative to sit the exam in his place, and not one of their tutors realised. What made it especially annoying was that Miles had been given top marks, and Jason had only studied climatology for a few months before dropping it for computer science.

But somehow it had worked. Jason was the brains of the family and Miles was the professional sportsman who was on the way to being world champion.

And that was okay. Hell—it was better than okay. The Gibson twins were the stars of the surfing world and Cory Sports went global.

Miles inhaled slowly and rolled his shoulders back as that cold icy feeling of dread welled up from the pit of his stomach.

Correction. That *had* been okay. Until the accident.

Now he was back in London to pretend to the

sporting world that it was business as usual for Cory Sports.

If only that were true.

Oh—he knew what the sports journalists were asking. Jason was at the helm and still one of the brainiest bachelors in London. But what about his brother? What was Miles doing in the business apart from learning to walk again? What future did he have when he stopped being the sporting hero? Good question. Pity that he did not have a smart answer for them. Not yet. But he would. He had to.

Sitting up taller, Miles decided to focus on something he could control and snorted in derision at the fawning press article before sending a suitable reply about how Jason's smart-boy haircut was bound to wow the ladies—if, *big if,* he ever found the time to meet any.

Jason was brilliant and had taken Cory Sports to places neither of them had ever expected.

But when it came to girls? Hopeless. No. Make that worse than hopeless.

His brother seemed to attract girls who either saw him as someone who they could get free sportswear from, or as a geek who they could persuade to run the IT in their companies in his spare time, then dumped him when they found out that he did not have any spare time.

Or then there were the worst kind. The professional gold-diggers who were happy to pursue any man who could even vaguely be described as a millionaire. Or, in their case, multimillionaire, although Jason would be the last person to brag about the money.

And Miles knew all about gold diggers.

Lori had been in his life for three years and not once did it cross his mind that she was using him and his status to get where she wanted to be. He was actually deluded enough to believe that she wanted to be with the real Miles Gibson, when in fact, she had a lot more interest in how he could further her career.

But when he had the accident? Well. He had stopped being useful to her any more and she had moved on to the next world-class sportsman who could give her the A-list profile she wanted. Having her own TV show was just part of the perks of that celebrity world.

And so was being invited to the Sports Personality Award show next week.

Which made it even more important that he walk into that sports event, on his own two feet, with a new woman on his arm and a twinkle in his eye.

The twinkle he could manage on his own.

But the woman? He wanted the right woman. Not another lingerie model like Lori.

No—he needed a stand-in date for one night— and just one night—who could hold her own.

A date with spark and energy and her own life and independence who could guard his back when he showed the world that Miles Gibson was not going to let a car accident stop him doing what he wanted.

Moaning to Jason that he did not want to go solo to the sports personality event had been a mistake. The last thing he had expected Jason to do was set him up on an Internet dating site. And he hated it when Jason got it so right. Andy was interesting. Funny. Oblivious to the fact that her real personality was there in every line of the emails that she had sent.

She had been worth coming out on a wet November evening.

All he had to do was turn on the charm and talk her into coming with him to the event. Done deal.

Suddenly there was a bustle of activity and Andy breezed past him, picked up her coat from the back of her chair, slipped it on without saying a word, and slung her bag over one shoulder.

He was just about to say something when she turned towards him, and the words stuck in his throat. Her skin was as white as paper, and from the quivering mouth it was obvious that she was upset about something.

Over him? Damn. Those girls must have got to her. Kissing her just to make an impression had been a big mistake, even if it had been the highlight of his day.

'It was very nice to have met you, but I need to head back. Urgent business. Thank you very much for the dinner and best of luck with the dating scene.' Then she gave a quick nod and turned away from him towards the door.

'Hey. Wait a moment,' he said, not wanting to draw attention to her, but if she heard him she pretended not to, and in one smooth motion flicked her collar up, flung open the door and strode away into the rain as fast as her legs could carry her. And was gone.

Miles stood up and tried to move after her, but he had been sitting in the one place too long again. His leg instantly cramped up and the pain in his knee switched from being just tolerable to pass-the-painkillers so quickly that he had to sit back down and massage the injured muscle back into life.

Well, this day got better and better.

He had just driven away the only online date he had agreed to meet.

And then he spotted something purple and umbrella shaped propped up next to her chair.

Saffie's house was in complete darkness when Andy walked up the path and turned the key in the front door. The rain had turned into a driving sleet and as the warm air hit her face and ears she could feel her cheeks tingle from the icy blast.

She had already been halfway down the street before she realised that she had left her purple umbrella back in the coffee shop—probably hidden below Miles's jacket. So she had waited for the bus that never came. So then she had gritted her teeth and walked for twenty minutes in her smart boots rather than just stand there and wait.

Waiting was for losers. Miles would never have waited—and neither would she.

Because standing on her own at that freezing bus stop with the rain running down her neck and inside her boots Andromeda Elizabeth Davies had come to a major conclusion. After twenty-eight years on this planet she had done enough waiting for other people in life.

She had waited for her parents to stop working just long enough to pay her some attention.

She had waited for someone to explain why they had to move out of her home and her own room with her own things into the hastily rearranged study of her grandparents' apartment, which she would be sharing with a lifetime of hoarded unwanted clutter.

She had waited for her parents to stop telling her how lucky she was to go to the private boarding school that was soaking up the trust fund her parents had started when they were rich and had money to throw away.

And then she had waited for her school friends to realise that she was just the same girl, only without any money. Saffie and her close pals had been brilliant but the others like Elise had dropped her in a week.

She had been prepared to wait for Nigel to make the first move and start dating her properly. Too busy with the project work, he had said. The presentation to the board for the new promotional plans for the coming year had to be perfect—but then they could relax and spend a weekend away together and tell the other people in the office that they were a couple. Surely she could wait a few more weeks?

She was his guilty little secret.

Sordid. Dirty. Expendable—and something he would simply throw away when he had used her enough. So he could get back to the girl he was living with.

Well, that was then and this was now. And she had waited long enough.

Meeting with #sportybloke Miles that evening had shown her just what she had been missing in her life—and it hurt that she did not feel able to open her heart to relax and enjoy his company as though it were a real date.

Because it had never been a real date, and she

had to remember that. No matter how lovely his smile, his touch and the feeling of his lips on hers.

Slipping off her wet coat, she strolled slowly up the staircase, her feet dragging and her wet boots feeling like lead weights on her feet. Each tread of the old wooden staircase creaked as she put her weight on the boards and echoed around the tall empty hallway, but she had become used to each familiar sound in this comfortable family-sized home. Her faithful friends were the chiming of the grandfather clock in the hall and the faint clanking from the central heating as it tried to bring some warmth to so many unoccupied rooms.

When Saffie had asked her if she wanted to come and keep her company, Andy had jumped at the chance to share a house with a girl she was proud to call her friend.

But that was two years ago, when Saffie was working in London and she could jump on a bus and be at the restaurant in twenty minutes. Now she was in Paris and not even a fast train link could make the distance any smaller.

Andy looked up at the stained-glass window at the top of the stairs. In summer the house was filled with coloured light and seemed a magical place, bright and positive and bursting with life.

But at that moment, it was dark, wet and windy and the rain lashed against the stained-glass and the only light was from the street light outside streaming in from the glass panel over the front door.

And as she stood there on the staircase, halfway to the landing, a huge weight suddenly seemed to press down on her shoulders.

Andy slid sideways onto the stair with her back against the wall as though the events of the day were too heavy to carry any longer.

She let her head drop back and just sat there, listening to the sound of her breathing and gentle sobs in the darkness.

It wasn't the dark, or the silence.

No, it was the crushing feeling of loneliness that drove her to feel sorry for herself. She had never got used to being so lonely. There was no one she could talk to about her life and her problems. Nobody understood her or was truly interested in her life.

Saffie was the nearest thing she had to a family. It would be the middle of the dinner service in

Paris around now, so she couldn't talk to her best pal until the morning—and Saffie worked so hard, driven by her passion for food to be the best she could be, and Andy admired her for that.

Goodness knew, Saffie could have trained as a lawyer as her parents wanted her to, but that wasn't what she wanted and she had started at the bottom washing dishes and ended up with a first-class degree in catering and a chance to show what she could do in a serious restaurant in Paris.

And nobody was prouder than Andy.

Saffie had been her best friend at boarding school when her parents were working silly hours in the city and sending the chauffeur to pick her up on a Friday afternoon. But what made her truly special was that Saffie had stuck by her even when the stock market exploded and her father's bank went under. Helping her friend out while finding somewhere else to live had seemed a brilliant solution to two problems. Win, win, as Nigel would have said.

Nigel.

Andy pressed her hand to her mouth, and then wiped away the tears from her cheeks.

Oh, what a fool she had been.

It had been the right decision to resign from her nice clean office job once she understood that he already had a girlfriend. No. Make that a rich girlfriend. The boss's daughter. There was no going back from that. Even if it had meant leaving a full-time job to work part-time for Elise to pay her bills.

It was just—sometimes she felt that she could touch the silence in this house which was more than her home—it was where she had her studio.

A small smile creased her lips and Andy blinked away her tears and sniffed.

Yes. She had her painting and her studying—and that was enough for anyone.

Maybe Miles was having a bad influence on her? Now there was a true entrepreneur who acted first then asked for permission later. What had he said? He took a chance. A risk.

She had been snatching an hour here and there over the past few months to work on what Saffie called her secret squirrel passion. Illustrating. The one thing in this world she would love to do more than anything else. That was why Nigel's betrayal hurt so much. She had sacrificed the time she could have spent on her true passion for him.

A man like Miles would never have put up with him.

Lesson learnt. Not again. Never again. No more waiting. No more putting it off until later.

Andy wrapped her hand tightly around the bannister and was just about to pull herself to her feet when her mobile phone rang out from her bag.

Saffie! She scurried around in her bag, terrified that she would ring off before she found her phone in the near darkness of the hall, and flicked it open, instantly creating a bright panel of light. Her shoulders slumped down in disappointment. It wasn't her friend. It was an email.

Then she froze. What if it was from Nigel?

Hardly daring to look, she quickly scanned down the list.

It was the online dating agency. #sportybloke had sent her a message.

Drat. Closing Elise's account was on tomorrow's list of things to do.

Exhaling slowly, she paused for a second before clicking on the email. He must think that she was a total idiot, running out on him into the rain like that without even a decent explanation.

Then her eyes widened and she sat back on the

stair and looked through the stair rails to the hall before reading the message again.

From: #sportybloke
To: #citygirl
Hi Andy.
Hope that you managed to dodge the rain and are not working too late.

I wanted to apologise for my rash act in the coffee shop this evening. Kissing you in front of the office gossips was neither tactful nor courteous. I do hope that it does not complicate things.

After you left I found a purple flowery umbrella which might be yours.

If you can stand it, I would like to meet you again and return your property in person.

You said in one of your emails that you like modern European food, and I happen to know about a new Spanish restaurant which has just opened in Soho.

How about dinner? Thursday. 7.30pm. Looking forward to it.

Say yes. Miles.

P.S. They have good cheese.

Andy stared at the screen, put down the phone and pressed her hand against her mouth, her mind buzzing with questions and options and excuses.

This was her get-out clause.

All she had to do was to thank him politely for the invitation and tell him that it hadn't worked out. Sorry. Best of luck. And that would be it. Job done.

She put the phone down on the stair and rubbed both of her hands across her face, then back over her hair to her neck. Her fingers massaged her neck for a few minutes, her eyes closed.

Nigel had deceived her. Tricked her. Used her for his own advantage.

And then she had done exactly the same with these online coffee dates. She had lied in every one of the many emails she had sent for Elise.

This was so wrong it was not funny. So many lies.

Well, that was over now. She was done with being used by other people who lied to her.

These men deserved better. Miles deserved better. A lot better. He had been nothing but nice to her and he was even more of the man she had imagined from his emails.

Andy read the message again on the brightly

lit screen that was illuminating her small strip of staircase. And the more times she read it, the more clearly the hidden message screamed out at her.

This was a pity date.

Miles felt sorry for her. Sorry for kissing her. Sorry for the trouble he might have caused. Sorry for being a nuisance—so he offered her a meal out as an apology which would make him feel better. He wasn't interested in her. Not really.

Her fingers moved over the tiny keyboard with the only answer possible.

To: #sportybloke
From: #citygirl
Hello Miles.
Thank you for your message but there is no need to apologise.

Spanish food sounds wonderful, and I am deeply flattered by your kind invitation, but I don't think seeing each other again would be a good idea. Hope that you enjoy your time in London. And best of luck with the online dating.

Please keep the umbrella. I think it would suit you.

Andy.

P.S. I love cheese.

Her finger hovered over the send button before she pressed hard down and watched the message go off into the ether.

Finished. Over. Done.

Andy pulled herself to her feet and inhaled deeply before lifting her leg and moving forwards. One step at a time, girl. One step at a time. Time to feed Saffie's goldfish Madge and relive a kiss from a sporty bloke that for a few brief moments had made her world a much brighter place.

CHAPTER FOUR

From: saffie@saffronthechef
To: Andromeda@ConstellationOfficeServices
Subject: Moment of madness

Hiya Gorgeous—thanks for the update. And for the good news about Miles—your hunky sporty bloke. Now we're talking. And I still cannot believe you turned him down!

Here's an outrageous idea. Track down this Miles and tell him that you have changed your mind and would LOVE to go out for dinner so that he can feed you cheese then dance the flamenco with a rose between his teeth. Tight pants and all. [I shall require photos]

What you need is a large dose of Aunty Saffie's famous remedy for getting over a rubbish relationship. Have a fling! Throw caution to the wind, raid my wardrobe for glad rags and go out and let your hair down and have some fun.

Otherwise I have this sneaky suspicion that you

will be sitting hunched over your drawing board for days on end. Don't do it.

Anyhow. Must dash. Or I will be in mucho troublo.

Have fun. Saffie

P.S. I mean it. Put down that pen and ink, right now. And, yes, I know that I am bossy but that is why you love me. J

MILES sat up against the bed head and flicked on the bedside lamp, his lungs fighting for air, squinting against the light until he could see all around him.

Heart thumping, his skin shiny with sweat, he swung his legs over the side of the bed, onto the solid oak floorboards, and felt the slight roughness of the wood under his toes. Reassuring. Real.

It had been the same dream again.

A memory played out so many times it had become like a scene from a favourite movie. A video played over and over until the words and images were embedded in the subconscious. Until the reality was lost, and the dream took its place.

Miles looked around the room.

Where was he? *Focus.*

The Cory Sports building. Upstairs in Jason's penthouse apartment.

London, he was in London.

In a too quiet, too calm and way too white bedroom, which looked just like all of the hospital rooms he had got to know over the past eleven months. Only without the smell.

Air. He needed air! Action. Sound. Movement. Colour. Life!

A cold autumn dawn was trying to creep around the edges of the window blind at the patio doors and he tried to push himself off the bed.

But his knee did not like that idea one little bit, and he winced in pain and lay down flat again, his fingers crushed into fists of anger and frustration.

How long had he slept?

Miles squinted at the electronic gizmo with about twenty dials that Jason called a clock. Five hours. Maybe six. Not enough.

The latest physiotherapist had given him strict instructions to get off his feet as much as possible and give his knee some chance at recovery.

Yeah. Right.

Miles lay back, legs stretched out in front of

him, but the pain was too much to ignore and his right hand automatically rubbed his right knee.

When would he be able to block out that movie clip from his memory?

Probably never.

He could still hear the voices in his head.

Have you heard that Miles Gibson has been in a car accident? Now he really has lost everything, hasn't he? Poor guy. He won't ever get up on a board again. Must be hard not having any career left.

Well, they were wrong. And he was going to prove just how wrong they were, then prove it again and again until they got the message straight. Miles Gibson was back on his feet and the same man he had always been.

The Gibson family had built up Cory Sports on the strength of having world champion kite surfer Miles Gibson at the helm. They were a good team. But these were hard economic times and the competition was fierce. His family had sacrificed everything to make his dream of being a professional surfer a reality. They needed him to get up there and tell the world that he was back to stay.

He would not let them down. No matter how much it cost him.

He was a fighter. And that was what he should focus on now.

Fighting. Every hard-won step of the way. Fighting through the pain.

Miles scrubbed harder at his leg, trying to massage the blood back into muscles and joints.

He had spent most of the past week visiting specialists all over London and they had all come to the same conclusion. There were no magical treatments or remarkable new experts that he could fly in to save the day, no extra medical equipment he could buy or new procedures.

The brilliant surgeons who had pinned his left leg back together had taken one look at his right knee and done the best they could. But it was no good and they knew it. His career had ended inside a vintage sports car that was never intended to comply with modern safety regulations. There was no airbag, no protective roll cage. Just a few layers of metal between him and the road.

His life as a professional kite surfer was dead. Gone. Finished.

Twenty years of hard work and pushing himself

to be the very best in his profession. Over in an instant.

And he hated that. He hated it with a passion that very few things in this life could match. One of them required the kind of escort agencies that might give him some distraction in the short-term, but were a terrible idea at any time, and the other needed sea, surf, high waves, quality boards and acrobatic kites.

Problem was—he still actually needed his knee in some sort of working order to be able to walk. Anything to avoid being confined to a wheelchair again.

Miles stopped punching at the innocent headboard, sat up and scrubbed at his hair with his fingertips just as Jason stumbled into the room, wiping his eyes then blinking at Miles over the top of his spectacles.

'I heard yelling. You appear to be alone so it can't be the obvious. The old dream again?'

'Yeah. Sorry if I woke you,' Miles answered as Jason flopped down on the bed and pulled the pillow under his head.

'No problem.' Jason yawned. 'I need to get in early anyway. That pretty receptionist the agency sent over knows nothing about sports and still managed to crash our complete online ordering system yesterday, so that's my morning wasted on interviews. How about you? Back to the physio?'

'No. Not today. But one thing is for sure—I need to get out of this apartment. I don't know how you do it, Jase. Seriously. I had no idea it would be so hard to stay indoors for more than a few days at a time. I didn't have any choice in the hospitals but this office work is killing me. Don't you ever yearn for fresh air and a beach now and then? No?'

Miles sighed and shook his head. 'Cabin fever.' He scanned the room, then shrugged. 'Great apartment. But you might have added something in the way of colour? All I can see are plain cream walls and if I look out the window I see grey skies, greyer buildings and most of the people in this city could use some sun and a humour transplant.'

Instantly he thought of #citygirl Andy and broke into a smile.

'One more thing to add to that list of things to do, Jase. Email that online dating service and tell them that the coffee date was a hit but the lady has decided that Internet dating was not for her.'

'Oh, no,' Jason groaned. 'Do I have to call lawyers? What did you do this time?'

'Relax, I didn't do anything unusual.'

'That's what I'm afraid of.' Jason inhaled sharply and lifted his chin. 'Hit me with it. Was she ancient, desperate, frigid or a gold-digger?'

Miles thought for a moment and did a rerun of their conversation, especially the part when she confessed that she was a stand-in for her boss. 'None of those things. Andy was different, cute. Although I'm not totally surprised that she didn't want to see me again seeing that…I might have, maybe, possibly…'

'Bro. Out with it. You didn't strip off in the middle of the restaurant to impress her with your tattoos or abs again, did you?'

'Worse. I embarrassed her in front of a couple of girls she used to know. She ran off before I could apologise. And there may be photographs.'

Jason winced. 'And you are supposed to be the ladies' man in the family. Well, our press cuttings agency will pick up anything that hits the gossip columns. What does this Andy look like?'

Miles conjured up an image of a girl with delicate cheekbones, silky fine brown hair curling at her ears and full pink lips, which had made one Panini the highlight of his day, and chuckled.

'Brunette. Green eyes. Dainty. Sassy in a suit. Doesn't freak when she drops food on her top and knows first aid. Nice hands. And she likes cheese.'

'Hands. Sassy. Cheese. Got it,' Jason said, slipping off the bed and polishing his spectacles on his tee shirt.

'You like this Andy, and don't try and deny it. Usually the only thing you are interested in is how she looks in or out of swimwear. I know you way too well. Pity you blew it.'

'What did I say?' Miles raised his arms in protest. 'You were the one who talked me into this online-dating game. All I need is a date for next week. One night. Not a relationship. End of story. And in case you have forgotten I am off the dating circuit and will be until further notice, remember?'

'I don't know why. Lori made her decision to dump you at the worst time possible. Fact. But that was months ago and you are more or less back on your feet. Another fact. You have been whining at me for weeks about having to find a date for the show. Don't blame me for taking the initiative.'

'Initiative? I'll give you initiative,' Miles growled. 'I am staying in this dull grey city long enough to show my face at the Sports Personality Award show, and then I am taking the initiative and getting out of the city to get some colour and spark back into my life. The Cory Sports roadshow hits Australia in less than eight weeks. Sun. Sea and surf. And it couldn't come soon enough.'

Andy grinned as a madcap bike courier jumped his cycle onto the pavement at breakneck speed, only feet in front of her, to overtake a stationary car, and then whipped back onto the road with a quick wave and was gone.

Normally she would have taken a second to steady herself and call after him with a cutting critique of what she thought about his driving skills. *But not today.*

Today she was going to the museum to show her friend the shop manager her Christmas card designs. There were so many fabulous commercial cards on display—but hers were hand painted, personalised and based on her favourite designs in the illuminated manuscripts room.

This was it. This was what she had been working on in every spare moment over the past year or more. Experimenting with new ideas for colours and borders and working late into the night until she was happy with the final result.

And she was happy with her work. *Very happy.*

Plus it was a bright sunny November afternoon and she had only one more party invitation to deliver for Elise—and then she would be free. *Free!*

Which was most excellent.

It was such a lovely day that she had walked through Covent Garden and up towards Holborn through streets she had known all of her life. The trees still had some of their leaves and the deep russets, reds and golds were stunning in the pale late-autumn sunshine. Shop windows were bright and bursting with colour from their displays of Christmas gifts and decorations. She had always loved autumn in the city. Especially when the sun was shining and she had the whole day ahead of her to enjoy.

Andy double-checked the address and map,

turned the corner through a high stone archway and stood quietly for a moment, admiring the stunning ornate architecture of the exclusive side street. Cory Sports had their London office in a converted four-storey stone Victorian building, which had been built when the British Empire was at its peak. Now the marble and glass entrance was modern and clean and welcoming rather than intimidating, but somehow it fitted in perfectly on this quiet pedestrianised area with its flower tubs and boutique shops and restaurants.

Elise had already paid her to hand paint the party invitations for her client's annual fundraising party in aid of high school art projects in London. Those A-list celebrities and senior business leaders expected a promotions company to send them a special invitation with a difference. Last year it was engraved crystal glassware—this year, hand-painted cards, each one designed to fit the person being invited.

No pressure, then.

Of course Andy would never tell Elise but she had loved every minute of this work. It was challenging, intricate and detailed. And she'd adored doing these pieces. But now they were done.

Thirty invitations. All personal. All hand drawn with the guest name written in calligraphy.

Cory Sports had been a special delight. It had only taken a quick glance at their online sales brochure to see that Cory was short for the Spanish word for the heart—Corazon.

Spanish. Perhaps she could have picked up a few more Spanish words if she had accepted the dinner invitation from Miles?

Andy gave a little chuckle. *Oh, Saffie. No flings for me. The last thing I need is another boyfriend.*

This was her time to make a new life for herself! And she could hardly wait.

Grinning from ear to ear, she only took a moment to leave the hand-embossed envelope with the friendly receptionist at the main desk, who promised faithfully to make sure that Mr Jason Gibson received the letter the moment he got back.

Tugging down her warm jacket, Andy stood outside in the warm sunshine, head back, her messenger bag across her body, and closed her eyes.

Finally! Now she could relax.

Except that as she dropped her shoulders and

inhaled, the most delicious aroma of freshly roasted coffee and baking filled her head and set her stomach growling.

Why not? The sun was shining, and she had just delivered the last VIP invitation. She could spare a few minutes to buy some lunch as a treat.

Strange how just the smell of that coffee took her straight back to the coffee shop and the way Miles had stirred his cup of coffee three times, clockwise, before taking a sip. She had never seen anyone do that before. Not adding sugar or cream, just stirring the grounds in the coffee.

He was such an interesting man. Pity that she would probably never see him again. Because the more she thought about him, and it was bizarre how often his face popped into her head, the more she wondered what he was really doing there that evening.

Of course she was flattered that he had come to meet her, the girl who had written to him, rather than Elise, but she was not stupid enough to think that a man like Miles would ever date her.

He was a chancer. A player. Turning on the charm to persuade a girl to provide some temporary amusement for him while he was in London.

And he had obviously done it before.

Well, not this girl. Not even if he was arrogant and bossy and funny and intriguing and all wrapped up in a gorgeous hunky package.

Shaking her head, she caved in and took the few steps across the street to the ornate French patisserie and coffee shop. Ah. *Temptation came in so many forms.*

Miles was just as luscious and bad for her health as the wonderful creamy cakes and pastries artfully arranged on glass shelves in the window.

Andy stepped into the shop with a skip in her step and a smile on her lips.

And froze. Her breath turning to ice in her lungs.

Because sitting at a corner table, laughing into the face of a glamorous blonde girl, was Miles.

Not that he was paying any attention at all to the customers waiting at the bakery counter.

Oh, no.

Miles was far too busy running the fingers of one hand up and down the blonde's arm, while the other hand rested on her knee. Her V-neck blouse had been designed to make the best of her substantial assets and he certainly seemed to be appreciating them. At very close range.

The blonde was wearing a very red short skirt that highlighted her perfect slim figure, high-heel red mules and had tanned bare legs that seemed to go on for ever. Her make-up was perfect, her long straight blonde hair salon sleek and overall she was just about as different from Andy as it was possible while still being in the same species.

Little wonder that he had now started to play footsie under the table.

Andy could have marched in playing the trumpet and Miles would not have noticed.

The cheek of the man!

Only a few days ago he had asked her out to dinner, and yet here he was, laughing and chatting up another girl in a coffee shop. And look at him! Short hair. Flash black business suit. Where had the sportsman gone?

She had been right all along. He was just another executive looking for a girl to adore him and tell him how marvellous he was. A chancer, pushing his luck in the hope that he would pick up some temporary female by dazzling them with his full-on charm offensive.

And if that blonde he was pawing was eating a Panini she would scream.

Andy glanced at their table. Of course. How silly of her. No carbs would contaminate that beautiful creature's lips.

Which only served to make her even more of a fool than she had been before.

This was the man she had been dreaming about every night, reliving his kiss and his gentle touch. While he had spent the time since they met on the lookout for his next date.

She had fallen for his little game. Which was so infuriating that she could hardly speak.

If there was any justice in the world, she should leap onto a table and denounce him to the world. But she wouldn't. There were limits to how much humiliation she was prepared to put up with, and she had already wasted enough time on this one.

Then her breath caught in her throat.

Miles pushed back his chair, whispered something to the glamorous blonde, who giggled in reply, then he stood up and started walking towards the counter.

Perhaps he had recognised her and wanted to warn her off?

But instead of scooting back outside, her feet felt as if they were glued to the floor and belonged to someone else, leaving her standing there like an idiot, staring at the shelves of baked goods as he casually strolled up and stood not more than a foot away.

And did not say a word to her. Nothing. Not even a curt hello.

In the second it took him to place his order for two more cappuccinos she gave him the once-over.

Someone who knew hair had given him the perfect tousled cut. The other evening his overlong dark chocolate hair had kept falling forwards but now it was smart city-boy short over his ears. With an edge.

He was wearing a black shirt, suit jacket and black trousers, which made him appear a lot slimmer and narrower in the shoulders. She could tell that it was expensive designer black, but he looked so different. Professional, businesslike and a lot paler than she had remembered. He must keep his rough-and-tumble charm and all-weather gear for outside work. Shame. Although she hated to admit it, she had liked that about him.

And he was still totally ignoring her. Which was more than rude.

'This is new,' she said to him in a low calm voice. 'I thought ordering from the table was more to your liking. Or have you decided to join the common people for a change?'

Miles turned to look at her with a smile, then glanced around as though looking to see who she could be speaking to.

'I'm sorry but I think you have the wrong person.' He shrugged, and then he added with a dismissive smile, 'I just have one of those faces,' and turned back to the counter where the barista was loading his coffees onto a tray.

What? Wrong person? One of those faces?

He turned and smiled at the blonde, and the penny dropped. Of course, Miles would not want his new date to think that he made a regular habit of meeting girls in coffee shops. No wonder that he was pretending that they had never met.

So she stepped forward and stood so close to him that their shoulders were touching, which seemed to startle him a little. 'I am so sorry about leaving so quickly the other night.' She swallowed down her nerves and gave a small cough. 'But thank you again for the dinner invitation.'

Miles looked at her with his mouth slightly open, blinked several times, then licked his lips and nodded slowly.

'I'm sorry. Have we met before? Which evening was this?'

The barista chose precisely that moment to bring the second cappuccino to the bar and must have overheard what Miles said because he instantly covered a snigger with his hand.

Brilliant. First Miles pretends he does not know her, and then even the barista starts sniggering at her.

She gave the barista a freezer glare, which sent him scurrying back to the coffee machine.

Come on, girl. Get it over and done with.

'Does online dating ring a bell? Monday evening?' she snapped, in a small, trembling voice, and lifted her eyebrows.

He stared at her with a tight closed mouth for so long that she wondered if he was okay, then suddenly Miles leant against the counter, his brows tight with concentration.

'Online. Right.' Then he nodded his head, just the once, his eyebrows headed skywards and he flashed her a polite smile. 'Of course. Andy. You have to be Andy. Well, I am delighted to see you, but, tell me, how did you manage to track us down?'

Andy closed her eyes and counted to ten but he was still looking at her when she blinked into his wide-eyed face. 'I am not a stalker. I haven't tracked you down and I didn't know that you would be here. Okay?'

She lifted her chin, straightened her back to try and gain another few inches and planted a hand on each hip. Suddenly furious. Miles didn't respect her—he didn't know how. He was just like all of the other people—just like Nigel—who had used her over the years, and then walked out and pretended that she was not important as a human being. And she was not putting up with that. For one more minute.

'I cannot believe that I actually wanted to apologise to you for the other night. Well, Mr hot surfing sportybloke, you can forget it. Forget that you kissed me, forget that you asked me out on a dinner date. In fact, it would be better if you forget that we ever met. And here is the drink I owe you, since you like water so much.'

And without thinking past the fury of the blood rolling in her veins, Andy picked up one of the water jugs brimming with ice cubes from the counter and poured the whole lot in one single gush all over the very startled head of the handsome idiot.

'Goodbye. We will not be meeting each other again.'

And with that, she clenched her teeth, turned on her heel and walked slap bang straight into a solid mass of man muscle.

'Well, that would be a real pity because that was the most fun I've had around here in a long time.'

It was him.

Right down to the hair and the attitude and the voice and a presence that made every other man in the room suddenly look smaller.

Andy reared back in shocked silence, opened her mouth to reply, then looked up into the face of the Miles she recognised from the coffee shop, and then back to the version who was still standing next to the bar, and then back to the man she was pressed up against.

Twins. *Identical twins.*

Oh, dear.

Her Miles lifted an eyebrow at her and, blast him, his gaze moved slowly from the tips of her comfy old green walking shoes to the red tartan beret she had chosen as a last-minute hat seconds before leaving the house to go to the museum.

She didn't like being trapped between this tall hunk of man and the solid wooden bakery counter. And she especially didn't like the fact that just looking at him, and inhaling his manly scent, had something pinging low in her belly.

It was just muscles, she thought in annoyance and frustration, and tried to stare him out.

Lunch. That was it. She needed lunch… At… the…museum.

She looked over at his twin, who was now being swabbed at with paper napkins by the glamorous blonde girl. His eyebrows were high and he was clearly waiting for an explanation as to why there were ice cubes in his hair.

She needed to get out of here.

'Wait a minute.' She blinked, trying to be casual. 'Whose date was I on last week? Yours—' she thumped him on the chest with the heel of her hand, which only made her hand sore and he didn't even blink '—or—' her fingers waved towards the man with the coffees '—the other yours?'

The suit coughed and tugged at the surfboard cufflinks in his tailored slim-fit black shirt before picking the ice cubes off his lap and stretching one arm out. 'Miles, over to you,' he replied.

The only sign that he felt even the tiniest bit guilty was a slight bunching of his jaw.

Andy whirled back to muscle man and her brain made the connections at lightning speed.

Go for it.

She took a breath and her words came tumbling out. 'I was honest with you from the start. I am not, and never have been, a stalker.'

She held her breath, not knowing what Miles would do.

'So just what are you doing here? Andy?' he asked, and took a step closer, so that her back was pressed against the counter. His hands were pushed inside the pockets of his cargo pants and he looked annoyingly casual and in control.

'Well, I certainly didn't come looking for you,'

she snapped. 'But if you must know, I have been making a delivery to the office across the street.'

He glanced quickly through the coffee shop window, then back into her face and then inhaled sharply through his nose. 'Do you mean the Cory Sports office? I'll take that look as a yes. So are you a messenger service?'

'No! Well, yes, but no.' She shook her head. 'Elise asked me to help her organise a fundraiser event and I painted the invitations myself.' She pointed to the office. 'I didn't want it to get lost in the mail so I delivered it myself. Okay?'

'So now you're an artist as well as a personal assistant and a messenger girl?' he asked in a voice of molten chocolate spiked with hot chili.

'Oh, that is just for starters. I have so many talents it's hard to keep up,' she answered in a low hoarse voice, her eyes locked onto his. And this time she had no intention of looking away first.

The air was so thick with electricity between them she could have cut it with a knife. Time seemed to stretch and she could see the muscles in the side of his face twitching with supressed energy, but she was not going to give in.

'My, it's awfully hot in here,' the suit said as

he stepped in front of his brother, breaking their connection and creating a space just large enough for Andy to step through, fully aware that she was still being glared at.

'Apologies for the misunderstanding.' The suit sighed, brushing the water from his trousers. 'That explains a great deal.' Then he stretched out his wet hand and shook hers as if he were about to hold a business meeting.

'Jason Gibson. Cory Sports. It appears that you have already met my brother, Miles. Delighted to meet you, Miss…'

Andy shook Jason's hand and tilted her head to one side, determined not to take the bait. 'Cory Sports? Ah. Fancy that. Enjoy your coffee.'

And with that she tugged the strap of her bag higher onto her shoulder, darted out of the patisserie, turned and gave the two men with the same faces who were both standing there, watching her, a small one-handed finger wave before the ornate painted glass door closed behind her.

Jason rocked back on his heels for a second before sniffing and glancing at Miles.

'You kissed her? And set up a dinner date?'

'Yes. And yes. I thought Mayte's new place.'

'Good choice,' Jason replied, with a nod towards the door. 'You had better get after her, then. Because, brother, I think you may have just met your match and you still need a date for the sports awards. Maybe there is something in this online dating after all?'

CHAPTER FIVE

MILES winced with pain from his knee as he half jogged across the cobblestoned side street. He had a cane back in the apartment but he would be damned before he used it in public… But the agony was worth it, because Andy was still waiting to cross the busy main road, her gaze focused on the contents of the messenger bag across the chest.

'Andy—wait up,' he called.

Her head shot up like a meerkat and she looked from one side to another before half turning back towards him. Instantly her shoulders slumped and she sighed and shook her head in disbelief.

'What? Have I not embarrassed myself enough for you for one day?'

She lifted both hands in the air and pretended to surrender. 'Okay. I admit it. I faked being Elise when I wrote those emails to the dating agency. There. Done. Can I get back to my life now please?

I hope you have better luck with the other lucky ladies.'

She glanced at her watch and winced. 'Lovely to chat but I need to be somewhere. Bye.' She turned on her heel and lifted her chin as she strode out into the sunshine. Opaque black tights. Green laced flat shoes. A navy padded jacket above a preppy red tartan swing skirt with a matching beret.

Her outfit was bright, colourful and in his eyes looked as sexy as anything. Correction—she looked as sexy as anything. What had he told Jason? That he was looking for some life and colour to make London bearable?

Well, he was looking at the perfect example right now. In the shape of a girl who had made him laugh not once, but twice. And that took some doing.

He hadn't met a girl as open and expressive as Andy for a very long time. If anything she was too open. Too honest.

Miles slowed his pace.

The self-protection mechanisms he had built up after Lori dumped him were still there, at the back of his mind, reminding him that he had made the same mistake with her. He had believed her, trusted her, shared his dreams and goals, given her everything. *Everything.*

And she had turned out to be just one more charming, beautiful gold-digger who was happy to be with him for as long as he was useful to her.

So why was he chasing a girl down a London street when his self-defences were screaming that Andy almost seemed to be too good to be true?

Well, there was only one way to find out. No way was he going to let Andy escape that easily. Not without her last name and a phone number.

He needed a date for one night.

And one night only. Not a relationship. Not a lover. A date. And Andy could be exactly the breath of fresh air that he had been looking for.

She marched ahead, totally engrossed in the busy traffic, and only stopped to glance behind her as they stood on the pavement waiting to cross the street. Andy whirled around to face him, her brows squeezed together, hands planted firmly on each hip. 'Are you following me? There are laws against that, you know. Are you really so bored?'

'I might be, or I could just be walking along, enjoying the fine weather.' He whistled casually.

'And I am not bored in the least. In fact, my day has suddenly become a lot more interesting. It isn't often that someone gets the better of Jason Gibson.'

'Right.' Then she ran her fingers back through her hair, slipping off her beret. 'Look, Mr Gibson. I have already apologised for the pretence. Elise had to go overseas at the last minute and she really did not want to reschedule the coffee date. But I made a mistake. I…I should have insisted that she write her own emails to the guys she was interested in…I was interested in. Oh, you know what I mean.'

'Ah. So you *were* interested in me?' He nodded. 'Pleased that we got that misunderstanding cleared up. And l am glad you were. Otherwise we would never have met face to face. Your emails were… interesting. Intriguing, even. I enjoyed reading them.'

Andy flicked her tongue out and licked her upper lip and suddenly the late-afternoon sunshine got a lot brighter. 'People don't realise just how much of themselves they reveal in these emails. I…was expecting someone different. More executive and less…' she flicked her fingers towards him '…athletic, I suppose.'

'Right back at you, girl. Maybe I was expecting someone different as well. And we both made a mistake. So here is an idea. Why don't we call a truce? And it's Miles, remember?'

'A truce?' she replied, her gaze scanning his face much longer than he had expected. Whatever she was looking for, she must have found it, because slowly, hesitantly, she nodded. 'If I say yes, will you stop stalking me, because I really do have a business meeting to go to? And it's important to me.'

'Say yes, and I promise not to stalk you. Okay?'

She exhaled slowly, then stuck out her hand and they shook on it. 'Truce it is. Now. Have a lovely day, Miles. See you around.'

And then she was off—practically skipping ahead.

But he was in luck—the traffic lights turned to green just as she tried to cross the road. Giving him the chance to catch up.

But then his luck ran out. Because driving down the small London street was a vintage English sports car, which looked so familiar it took his breath away in shock.

He closed his eyes for a second and he was back inside his beloved little red sports car. His dad had bought it second-hand from a friend in Cornwall, and the two of them had worked hard to restore it with loving care in the family's tiny draughty wooden garage just in time for his seventeenth birthday. He had done the heavy lifting and his dad had supplied the technical knowhow.

It had been his first real motor and the envy of every other boy in the school. Even Jason, who had never shown any interest in cars and opted for a home computer for his seventeenth instead.

He had loved that car. Loved just taking off to the beach for the day, during the school holidays or a family picnic on a summer Sunday.

It had taken him three days to drive it down to Spain and take the ferry across to Tenerife—but it had been worth it to have his own car. Sunshine. Top down. Classic.

And it had never let him down. Not once. And then he'd had to listen to every sound it made as it was crushed and wrecked beyond repair by a drunken truck driver. With him still inside. Together to the end.

He could recall every aspect of that morning in full colour.

The car radio had been playing classic songs from the sixties. The sun was shining. The road was clear. In the dream memory, the unreal Miles knows that something is about to happen, and even though the next few minutes have played themselves over and over again in the past months Miles still cannot avoid the inevitable. He is powerless to do anything to change it. He becomes a passive observer, just watching, as the traffic lights change to green and he engages first gear and moves slowly forward before changing into second.

And then the soundtrack changes. Metal being crushed. Bags and loose papers and sports kit flying around from side to side, the horizon spinning around, over and under the car before it stops rolling and smashes back down to rest on its side.

He remembered leaning, half suspended from his seat belt, his lower body trapped below the hips. And someone was screaming. And was still screaming when the ambulance and police arrived and he realised that he was the one doing the screaming.

Miles forced open his eyes into the real world that was London in November.

He knew what would happen next. He had to control his breathing. Come on, he knew the routine. Deep breaths right down to the abdomen.

Forget the fact he couldn't even drive. And seeing that car killed him all over again.

Time to wake up and live. Wasn't that what all of those doctors had told him to do? Focus on the positive. Focus on the fact that most of him was still functioning and by some fluke and good safety belts he had escaped a head injury?

Miles glanced around and took his bearings. Andy was still standing at the pavement.

She was as good a place to start as any. He had a new goal.

'Not so fast, girl. I'm not used to being turned down, so I have to wonder. What was the real reason you decided to turn up in the place of your boss the other night? Just curious. Not stalking. Curious.'

'Curious?' she replied as they walked across into a wide piazza in front of an impressive stone building, but he could hear a supressed smile in her voice. 'Well. What a coincidence.'

'Isn't it? My biggest failing. Can't help it. Was it just for the money? Or were you wondering what I looked like? In the flesh, as it were.'

She stopped and scowled at him. 'Yes and maybe. But mostly I did not like the idea of you just sitting there on your own waiting for a girl who is never going to show up because she is in Brazil and has changed her mind. And you. Are an incorrigible pest. Do you know that?'

'Hey. Flattery. I am a businessman,' Miles replied, then stopped and gave her a small nod. 'Thanks for taking the time to turn up. It was sweet. But you need not have worried. I don't wait for girls. And I will not be thwarted. That dinner invitation still stands.'

Her reply was to sigh low in her throat and walk towards a huge arched stone portico that formed the entrance to the building. She gestured to a large marble plaque on the entrance with the words 'The Harcourt Collection' engraved onto the surface in gold lettering.

'Far too busy. Busy, busy, busy.'

'I'll wait. Where are we headed?'

'This is one of the finest museums in London, and my favourite place in the whole world. I also happen to work here at weekends. So the staff know me and I would be mightily miffed if someone—' and she lifted her eyebrows high '—was to diss me once we get through these doors. So if you can't agree, maybe we should say our goodbyes here.'

Miles blinked at the plaque a few times. *A museum? She worked in a museum? Well, this got more bizarre and intriguing by the minute.* Maybe she was as multitalented as she claimed.

Andy turned to go but he stepped in front of her.

'Not so fast. I don't get to London very often. I didn't even know this place existed. It would be a shame to miss the chance to see what it looks like on the inside. In fact, seeing as you know the museum so well, how about a guided tour?'

'A tour? No. Sorry. I have to plan my sales pitch before the meeting and calm down on my own. I need this quiet time to myself. But if you ask at the information desk I am sure that you could join the next tour. Tourists are always welcome.'

Miles growled at her through narrowed eyes. 'Nice try. Not going to work. But you mentioned those magical two words, sales and pitch. Why didn't you say so? You act as my guide and I'll write your pitch for you. Deal?'

She glanced from side to side and swallowed before stepping closer to him so that she could reply in a harsh whisper. 'I don't mean to offend you, but I am an illustrator and I want to persuade the museum to sell my hand-crafted greetings cards through their shop.'

She lifted her right hand, palm up, and stared at it. 'Sporting goods.' Then she did the same thing with her left hand. 'Illustrated greetings cards.' She stared at one hand, and then back to the other. 'Note the difference.'

Then she dropped both hands and stared up at the imposing entrance. 'This is me sticking my neck out and taking a chance and I am rather nervous so thank you but no. I need a moment on my own.'

Her long dark eyelashes fluttered close to her smooth pale cheek as she dropped her head, eyes closed, her chest rising and falling below her jacket as she took several calming breaths.

And every cell of his body twanged to attention.

Either this girl was an extraordinary actress or his instincts had been right and she was someone worth getting to know.

Time to switch up a gear and clinch his date for the night.

Miles chuckled and grabbed her hand. 'You haven't heard my pitch yet. Take the risk. You won't regret it.' And in one smooth motion he flung open the heavy embossed door and stepped inside, dragging Andy with him, complaining loudly all the way.

'And you really think that I can ask that much for each card?' Andy asked as they strolled out of the collection of eastern jade and porcelain.

'Absolutely,' Miles replied, his eyes focused on one of the Christmas card samples that Andy had brought with her. 'You haven't taken account of your hourly rate. This is excellent work and beautifully painted. Offer the museum the cut I suggested and you both benefit—but don't undervalue your workmanship. People pay for quality—I know I do. And you have already customised it for this outlet.'

'I hadn't thought of it that way. But the inspiration did come from this museum.'

Andy pointed to the central gold-and-blue design on the card he was holding. 'Each central motif is based on a letter from a medieval illuminated manuscript, which are so wonderful it is hard to put into words.'

She paused, gave a quick nod and pointed to a room just down the corridor and flashed him a grin that made him blink. 'Actually it's easier to show you than try to describe it. The books and documents are in here.'

Miles followed on as fast as he could but he had been on his pinned and dodgy legs for way too long so that Andy was already crouched over a long glass display cabinet when he joined her.

And then she looked up at him.

And the transformation on her face was so miraculous that he was taken aback by it.

Her whole body seemed to have come alive, so that her eyes sparkled with life and energy and when she spoke her voice was completely different.

It was as if something had flicked a switch inside this girl.

This version of Andy was bursting with enthusiasm and excitement and joy.

He knew that look. He had seen it before.

It was the look of someone with the fire in their belly that burned hot with the passion of doing the one thing they loved most in the world.

A passion that nothing else in life could replace or come close to matching.

And he knew exactly what that felt like.

A cold hand clasped around his heart.

Would he ever feel that passion again? That glow that beamed out from Andy's face at that moment when she looked at these books with the coloured pages?

He envied her that. More than he could say.

Bitter bile at the injustice of what had happened to him roiled deep inside, but he pushed it away. Not her fault. It was his job to deal with the fact that his world had shifted.

There was a good chance that he would never stand on a surfboard again or feel the rush of a kite lifting his body high above the waves. Not if he wanted to walk or live his life without wheelchairs or canes.

One thing was certain.

This kind of passion could never be faked or copied.

She was the real deal.

Not an actress or someone out to con him—but someone who was as passionate about these handwritten and decorated books as he had been about his sport.

Was this what he had glimpsed between the lines of those few emails that she had sent him? He had certainly sensed that there was something special about her, but passion like this? No. This was a bonus.

But it was more than that. The Andy he had met in the café was pretty and sassy, but this Andy was transformed by her happiness and joy into a very remarkable woman who was intent on telling him all about the royal families who had commissioned these hand-painted books in a world before the printing press had been invented. Her expertise and knowledge streamed out of her.

Andy was not just pretty. This Andy looked stunningly beautiful.

And right there and then, he made the decision.

I want you to look at me with that passion in your

eyes. I want you to warm my cold disappointment at the fire of your passion while I have the chance.

This one. I choose this one.

Heart thumping, he could barely drag his gaze from her face to the pages she was describing.

Andy leant her elbows on the frame around the glass case and sighed in wonder at the pages of the book on display.

'Isn't it astonishing?' she said and her shoulders seemed to drop several inches as she grinned up at him, her eyes sparkling with fire and happiness and delight.

Her joy was so contagious that Miles could not help but grin back and move closer, so that they could look down at the exhibit together.

His hand seemed to move to her waist all on its own and, judging by the instant flash of a grin she gave him, the lady was not complaining. She was having way too much fun.

While Andy's gaze was totally locked onto the beautiful manuscript, Miles took the time to look at her close up. In the natural light her hair was not brown but a blend of every shade of gold and brown with copper and russet blended in. Lori used to spend the cost of a new surfboard on having her hair coloured and it had never even been close to this fabulous.

It hurt him to think that Andy had no clue about how very naturally beautiful and gifted she was.

He moved closer and pointed to the left page where a giant bird in the shape of the letter P had been covered with the most intricate and startling of ancient circles and birds and flowers and animals.

'Tell me about how they made those colours. And is that real gold?'

'The colours?' she replied, blinking up at him and clearly delighted that he was showing any interest at all. 'Oh, yes. This is real gold. This set of gospels was meant to be a royal gift so the monks had the very best of everything. The blue is azurite and lapis lazuli from Afghanistan rather than native indigo and that fresh green colour is most likely malachite. It truly is a masterpiece. And I love it so much. I could look at it all day.'

All day?

His leg was already complaining about walking about for an hour and he had just about reached his limit on his other knee.

He might have to ask the guard if he could borrow his chair.

Luckily he did not have to, because just as he was about to reply the sound of a herd of baby elephants echoed up from the stone staircase. He took a tighter hold of Andy and they both turned to see what all the noise was about—just in time to see an entire junior school of jostling, jabbering, running, curious and mega-excited children burst into the exhibition space. All desperate to be the first ones to see the books and all competing in decibels to get the attention of their already harried teachers.

Andy stepped back from her precious book with a sigh, looked up at Miles and shrugged.

'I have a suggestion.'

She glanced from side to side around the room. The way into the café area was blocked by the second wave of children, who all wanted drinks at that very minute, and they would have to fight their way back to the main exit. *Time for Plan B.*

'What would you say if I told you that I knew a secret exit onto the dome and we could escape the school party and read the guide book in peace?'

Miles replied by taking what was a surprisingly

firm hold around her waist, which made her gasp, before he whispered, 'I would tell you that I will follow you to the ends of the earth. But make it fast. The teacher is heading this way. And she has a clipboard.'

'Okay, now I am intrigued,' Miles whispered as they stood at the railing and looked out through the curved glass at the busy London street below. Above their heads was the curved dome of the ceiling of the museum, which was a masterpiece of metal and stone and arched beams, inset with decorated panels of stars and mythological creatures.

The walkway they were standing on ran the complete circle of the dome of the building and was a hidden gem, offering a complete three-hundred-and-sixty degree view over the entire city of London in all directions through the row of heavy glass wall panels.

The sound of clinking glasses and children's chatter and the noise from the buses and taxi cabs outside filtered into the space and yet they were quite alone. Separate.

'How on earth did you know about that secret staircase leading up from the exhibition?'

Andy looked up at him and her lips curled into a smirk before she replied. 'Oh, I have explored most of these corridors and they haven't changed at all. In fact...' and at this she paused. 'They are exactly the same as I remember them.'

Then Andy took pity on his confusion and she smiled and leant forward before adding, as casually as she could, 'I grew up in a house not very far from here. So you see, I have been coming to this museum all of my life.'

She stopped suddenly, dropped her shoulders back and pointed towards the ceiling. 'When I was little I had a copy of that zodiac in the ceiling of my bedroom so that I could lie in bed at night and watch them and dream about what they all meant. It was magical!'

'Your parents must have loved bringing you here,' he replied.

'My parents? Not exactly,' she answered with a shrug. 'They both worked in the city and they didn't have a lot of free time, even at weekends.'

Andy tilted her head and was grateful that his gaze was fixed on the window glass so that he could not see the glint in her eyes. Talking about those sad times still hurt.

'I had a series of au pairs and nannies who soon found out that they could take off to the café to chat and leave me to explore the exhibits.' Andy waved one hand, then let it fall as she turned back to face him. 'So when they weren't looking I took off to explore on my own. The curators and security guards soon got to know me and I never made a mess or got into trouble. This was my personal playground.'

'Wow,' he replied, with the look of something close to awe in his face. 'Are you serious? Did you really grow up wandering around in a museum?'

'Oh, yes,' she answered with a tiny shrug. 'And don't say it as though that was a bad thing. I loved it here. My folks eventually worked out that I was spending far too much time learning about ancient Persian history so they sent me to boarding school at the age of eleven. Too late, of course. By then the damage was done. I was a history geek and proud and nothing my parents told me about the advantages of a career in hedge funds was going to change my mind.'

His reply was a low snort of disbelief.

'Quite. No, I have wonderful memories of sitting up here all alone, dreaming about the wonderful research I was going to do and all of the ancient manuscripts that were still out there for me to explore.' Her voice faded slowly away as the contrast between her life and the life she had imagined for herself flashed into sharp focus. 'My life was going to be so magical.'

Miles must have picked up on her change of mood because he moved closer so that their coats were touching.

She instantly switched her smile back on. *Not his problem.*

'Now I have started some freelance PA work for my friend Elise and work on the information desk here on Saturdays but we are always mad busy. This is a rare treat.'

'That is because you love this place so much and you miss it,' he replied in a gentle voice, and chuckled at her gasp of surprise. 'Yes. It is fairly obvious. Especially…'

'Especially?' Andy asked in a shaky breath. She was not used to opening up to a millionaire that she had just met in this way, and it startled her, and yet was strangely reassuring. *Weird.*

'I was going to say, especially considering that there must be so little work for history graduates.' He blew out hard and blinked. 'Research on ancient documents! That's hard for me to get my head around. It must be hard to do office work when you have such expert knowledge of the subject.'

Hard? How did she even begin to explain to a stranger the misery of having to turn down her place at a prestigious university, which she had worked so hard for, because there simply was not the money to pay for her parents' new business disasters at the same time as sending her to university? They wanted her to study for a degree that would guarantee her a secure future as a professional, not some ridiculous foolishness about art history. That was not going to get her anywhere. After all, she was not gifted or talented.

She had begged her grandparents to support her, and applied for grant after grant, but it had all been for nothing and in the end she had had to face the truth.

If she wanted to make the world of illuminated manuscripts her life, then she would have to do it with money that she earned.

Her whole world had shifted under her feet and was still shifting now.

Even after ten years of living in rented accommodation, and now as a house sitter, there were some days where she had to remind herself that she could still do it. She read and studied and practised her techniques, constantly working to become the best she could be. Evening classes. Museum workshops. Anything that would improve her knowledge and skills.

Andy blinked hard. The blur of constant activity that she used to fill each day created a very effective distraction, but even talking about those sad times brought memories percolating up into her consciousness. Memories she had to put back in their place where they belonged.

Then she looked up at the new moon rising in the clear sky above the tall stone buildings across the street and felt the sting of tears in the corners of her eyes as the memory of the lost opportunities flooded back into her mind. She was so overwhelmed that when Miles shifted next to her on the railing, she suddenly came crashing down to earth and the harsh reality that her life was so very different from the one she had imagined for herself as a girl.

'Oh, I am so sorry,' she said through a tight, sore throat. 'Here I am, rambling on about illuminated manuscripts and my boring life history. How embarrassing! I don't usually go on like this but this has been a tough week. But thank you for listening.'

Miles inclined his head towards her. 'I got the feeling that you needed to talk. Apparently I was right. And you were not boring, not in the least.'

Andy instantly whipped her head around to check if he was making fun of her, as Nigel had, as so many of the men she had met had. But instead of supressed ridicule, he was doing the laser stare through the centre of her forehead again. No laughter. Just something close to sincere curiosity.

And it totally disarmed her.

'Thank you,' she replied, then gave a small cough to cover her embarrassment. 'How about you?' Andy asked with a lift in her voice, eyebrows high. 'Where did you live growing up?'

'Ah. Nothing like this,' he replied with a chortle. 'I was born in Cornwall. My dad was a sports teacher so we spent most of our free time on the beach or helping him to run training sessions for local schools and colleges. But in the winter we went to my grandparents' beach house on Tenerife. Sunshine and surfing.'

Miles shrugged deeper into his down coat. 'I soon found out that Cornwall was amazing in the summer but in January? Technical surfing was a lot easier in the Canary Islands.'

'Oh, I so agree,' Andy said with a knowing nod. 'Technical surfing. Absolutely.'

'Even so,' Miles said as he moved closer so that he could stand next to her with his arms stretched out on the metal railing as they both gazed onto the London street, 'I envy you growing up here. There is something special about the city at this time of year.'

The tall London plane trees had been strung with white party lights and Christmas decorations so the front entrance of the hotel opposite looked like a fairy-tale picture of Christmas from a children's book.

Huge white plastic snowflakes, bright red-and-gold baubles and lots of silver-and-gold-dusted ivy dotted with crimson holly berries were suspended from wires to form perfect garlands and wreaths.

The shops along this busy high street had decorated their windows with wonderful displays of toys and gifts and the finest luxury goods to be had in the city in magical winter wonderlands of huge stores and designer shops and specialist food outlets.

And as Andy and Miles looked into the early evening dusk the first Christmas street lights twinkled bright and colourful and cheerful. Pedestrians hurried along, bundled up against the cold, children and adults smiling and enjoying the bustle and energy of the city street.

The whole scene was so familiar to her and yet still so magical that Andy felt her shoulders relax for the first time in many days.

This was why she'd never found peace when she had lived in boarding school or with her grandparents. They had never come close to this special place in her life.

She leant in contented silence and grasped the balustrade with both hands, quietly aware of how very close she was standing next to this man she had only just met. Close enough that she could hear his breathing and the sound his boots made as he shifted his weight from one foot to the next. The sharp tang of his aftershave combined with the dust and polish from a large building to create a heady scent.

Should she tell him that he was the first man that she had ever brought to the roof dome? Perhaps not. He had already teased her about being an online dating virgin.

But as she fixed her gaze on the thick glass panel, she knew that it was more than that.

Miles had come here to be with her—because he wanted to.

He even appeared happy to enjoy the view and remain in silence and allow her to do all the talking, since she was relaxed enough in his presence to enjoy the type of conversation that could only happen between strangers, unfettered by past history.

Strangers.

Tears pricked the corners of her eyes and she looked away from Miles out over the city.

Stupid! Why had she just told so much of her life to this stranger?

Miles wasn't her friend. *Far from it.*

She knew his laugh, his smile, the way he stirred his coffee, but she had no clue who he was or why he wanted to spend his afternoon in a museum with her.

This was Miles Gibson of Cory Sports. Multi-millionaire sportsman. Driven, intense and determined to succeed in the business he had built up with his brother.

Instinctively she felt the man in the black down coat looking at her, watching her, one elbow on the metal railing.

She turned slightly towards him and noticed for the first time, in the fading natural light and the twinkling stars in the street, that his eyes were not brown but a shade of copper the colour of autumn leaves. And at that moment those eyes were staring very intently at her.

On another day and another time she might even have said that he was more gorgeous than merely handsome. Tall, broad and so athletic it was a joke.

Dazzle factor and allure of this quality did not come cheap.

Some lucky girl was going to have a wonderful online date.

He took a step closer in the fading light and in the harsh shadows his cheekbones were sharp angles and his chin strong and resigned.

The masculine strength and power positively beamed out from every pore and grabbed her. It was in the way that he held his body, the way his head turned to face her and the way he looked at her as though she was the most fascinating woman he had ever met, and, oh, yes, the laser focus of those intelligent copper brown eyes had a lot to do with it as well.

He was so close that she could touch him if she wanted to. She could practically feel the softness of his breath on her skin as he gazed intently into her eyes. The background noise in the museum seemed to fade away until all of her senses were totally focused on this man who had outspokenly captivated her.

She couldn't move.

She did not want to move.

'What are you doing here, Miles Gibson? What do you want from me?'

CHAPTER SIX

HER words blurted out in a much stronger voice than she had intended, and she instantly warmed them with a small shoulder shrug. 'Your brother probably has a stack of work waiting for you back in the office. Shouldn't you be getting back?'

Miles straightened his back and lifted his chin before releasing the railing and turning to face her.

'What am I doing here? Well, I thought that was fairly obvious. Since you don't want to have dinner with me, I had to find some other way of satisfying that terrible curiosity I am cursed with. And, yes, he certainly does have a mountain of admin waiting for me, and, yes, I probably should, because my knee…' Then he pushed his lips out, licked the bottom one with his tongue and said in a clear calm voice as though he were reading from a script. 'Car accident. Still having physio.

Hurts when I stand. And we have been doing a lot of that this afternoon.'

'Oh, no,' she gasped and clutched onto the sleeve of his jacket as she looked down to his trousers. 'You should have said something. I am so sorry.'

'Not a problem,' he replied in a voice of finely sharpened steel that cut the air. 'I'm fine.'

She snatched up her head and stared into his eyes, shocked by the change of tone in his voice.

Whatever casual friendly atmosphere they had built up—was gone. Vanished into smoke. And it was as if a blast of ice-cold air had just blown into the dome, making her shiver.

She closed her eyes for a second, and when she opened them, she almost jumped back because Miles was standing so close to her that the front of his soft jacket was almost touching her sleeve.

'It was worth it to share another person's passion first-hand. And that is what you have, Andy. You have passion.' He sniffed. 'Takes one fanatic to recognise another one. So thank you.' He took another step closer, so that when she looked into his eyes she had to lift her chin to do it. 'For being my guide into another world I knew absolutely nothing about.'

And with one tiny nod he stepped back, his hands sliding up and down the sleeves of her coat. 'Come on, girl, it's getting cold up here. You're trembling. I'm taking you for a hot coffee. Tea. Whatever. And on the way I want to hear you practise your sales pitch. Shall we?'

He stuck out his hand and she looked at it for a fraction of a second. Taking his hand would mean saying yes to spending more time with him, the coffee, everything. But before she had a chance to think, he grabbed it firmly and laughed out loud. 'One more thing. I think it's about time you told me your real name. What does the Andy stand for?'

She hesitated for a moment before raising her gaze to the ceiling and blurting out, 'You had better not laugh—it's Andromeda. Andromeda Davies.'

He lifted his head and nodded. 'Andromeda. It totally suits you.'

He raised one fingertip and traced it along her cheekbone.

'And in case you were wondering—I know about dreams. So does Jason. Do you think we were handed Cory Sports on a silver platter? No.

We had to wash dishes and work weekends and school holidays to earn the money to buy the kit and teach and learn and teach and learn some more before we were even close to being ready to go professional. But you know the true meaning of the word amateur, don't you?'

He dropped his hand so that it rested lightly on her hip and she could feel the warmth and the weight of his fingers through several layers of fabric.

She shook her head slowly from side to side, speech impossible.

'It comes from the Latin word *amator*—the lover. Now a girl who loves what she does so much that she can keep the fire of her passion for history burning for ten years…that is a girl who I would like to know more about. See more.'

Then he kissed her on the tip of her nose. And the touch of his lips was as gentle as a butterfly landing and she closed her eyes to revel in that tiny moment when her skin was in contact with his.

'What do you say, Andromeda Davies? Are you willing to be seen in public eating Spanish food with me? Oh—and this time? This time it will be a real date. You and me. First-name terms. I would like to hear a lot more about those dreams of yours. Tempted?'

Tempted?

Andy stared into his face for a second in total silence, aware that she was probably ogling and looking as bewildered as she felt.

Of course she was tempted.

Had he no clue what he was asking?

Why could he possibly want to have dinner with her? To hear about her dreams? Listen to her plans and fantasy ambitions?

She had no fabulous stories of international travel and achievement to amuse a man like Miles. Did he feel sorry for her and the life she led? Or simply need someone to talk to because he was lonely? She didn't need that either.

Andy inhaled deeply, his gaze on her face as he waited for her answer.

But when he moved even closer, she took two steps back, away from the temptation—the danger.

Her heart was thumping so loudly he could probably hear it from where he was standing. He smelt wonderful, his touch sent her brain spinning and he was so handsome that her heart melted just looking at him.

She had felt that wicked pull of attraction in the coffee shop the other evening and run away. And she would have to do the same now, because the high-tension wire that was pulling her closer and closer towards Miles Gibson would only lead one way—to her heartbreak and pain.

She had learnt her lesson with Nigel and dared not place her trust in a man like this again. She just couldn't risk being used then cast aside.

She wasn't ready to date anyone. Nowhere near.

'A dinner date? Thank you, but I don't think that would be a very good idea, Miles. But perhaps Jason could find you another online date in my place?'

'Not a good idea?' Miles frowned. 'I don't know about that. The girl who runs it comes from our part of Tenerife and her whole family are terrific cooks. Mayte will look after us well. And no squishy tomatoes in sight.'

'Then that is a very good reason why I am the last person you should ask out as your date. A friend of your family might get the wrong idea.

And I am really not looking for another boyfriend at the moment.'

Miles paused for a moment, pressed his lips together, winced and then slapped the heel of his hand to his forehead as he took several steps back towards the entrance. 'You already have a boyfriend. Of course you do. It was your boss who needed the online dating agency.'

He gave her a short bow. 'Apologies. I jumped to conclusions. Another one of those flaws I was talking about. I only hope your boyfriend doesn't turn up at the office and thump me for asking his girl out. I'm not sure my brother could take any more surprises today.'

There was just enough of a change in his voice to make her look up. Unless he was a very good actor and she was completely misreading the signals, she saw a glimmer of genuine regret and disappointment cross that handsome face before he covered it up.

Interesting.

Decision time. Pretend she was seeing someone and lie through her teeth...or not.

'Jason is safe. What I meant was that I recently broke up with someone and I don't feel comfortable going on any kind of date just yet. But thanks again for the invitation.'

It was astonishing to see how fast Miles could switch on that killer smile.

'Ha. So you are single. That makes two of us.' He looked at her quizzically, eyebrows high. 'But you do know what that means, don't you?'

He stepped closer, ran his hands up both sleeves of her jacket and smiled as his gaze locked onto her eyes.

'I simply won't take no for an answer, Andromeda. Not going to happen.' And he winked at her. Just as he had done in the coffee shop the other evening. So smug and confident in his dazzling power. And with just the same power to make her roll her eyes and sigh out loud as she slithered out of his grasp.

'Which part of not wanting another boyfriend right now do you not understand, Miles? I appreciate the offer but I really am not ready for a new relationship—with anyone. So, thank you, but no.'

Then she patted the front of his coat briskly with her fingertips and gestured with her head towards the stairs, before glancing at her watch. 'And look at the time. I have been keeping you chatting for far too long. Thank you for keeping me company and for the kind advice about the pitch, but I think I had better put those tips to good use while they are still fresh in my mind.'

Andy stretched out her hand. 'Goodbye, Miles Gibson. And thanks for the business tips.'

Miles inhaled the heady atmosphere of the dusty museum and the light floral perfume that Andy wore and tasted the slight tang that came with the possibility that his fine plans were about to be scuppered.

She was serious! She was actually turning him down.

There had to be *some* way to persuade her to change her mind and agree to be his date. What did she want? There had to be something. And just as that thought popped into his brain she shuffled her shoulder bag higher and the corner of one of her greeting-card folders popped out of the top.

And then he had it.

Her artwork.

That was it. He was going to fuel the fire of her passion by offering her the one thing that could make a difference. Fire for fire. A date in exchange for her heart's desire. He knew that her passion would never allow her to turn down an offer like that.

His fingers closed around hers and his mouth curled into a warm smile as her smooth-skinned, cool, clever fingers moved against his. 'Thank you, Andromeda Davies, and it was my pleasure.' But instead of releasing her, he kept hold of her hand as though reluctant to let her go, and although she coughed and glanced down at her fingers he did not move an inch.

'You asked me earlier what I wanted from you, and do you know, I never did answer your question. How very rude of me. Do you still want to know my answer?' He paused, knowing that he had her full attention, then moved half a step closer and pressed a fingertip to her lips just as Andy was about to reply.

'One of the reasons I am in London is to attend the annual Sports Personality Award show. Cory Sports is the main sponsor. And I need a date for the evening. That's why Jason signed me up with the online dating agency.'

And he lifted his eyebrows and grinned. 'If you

don't want to eat dinner with me, how about going to the awards show as my date for the evening?'

'Your date at the sports awards? You? Miles Gibson?' Andy asked, her eyes wide with disbelief.

'Hell, yes. And only the best for you, girl. Top table all the way. From what I am paying that celebrity chef we should have a decent meal. Couple of glasses of wine. And if my memory serves me correctly you would be sitting next to that film actor who does his own stunts in the Bond movies. You know the one?' Miles sniffed. 'I shall take that squeak to be a yes. The athletes will want to talk sport but I am sure you can cope for a few hours before we hit the real party. What do you say? Are you willing to take a risk on having a brilliant time?'

'Are you on medication?'

'No…well, actually, yes. But only at night so I can sleep for a few hours.'

'Thought so. Miles, I don't know the first thing about sport. I hate having my photograph taken and I would probably be asleep with my head on the table after a couple of glasses of wine. This is not a good look when you are the sponsor and probably have several members of the royal family presenting awards. Thank you, but I am so *not* the girl you want to have as your date for a prestigious event like this.'

Miles was silent for a few seconds, his gaze flitting across her face. Then he took both of her hands in his, flashed a closed-mouth smile and tilted his head slightly to one side.

'Two royal princes, plus several radio and TV presenters. And as it happens, I would be honoured to have you on my arm for the evening.'

That seemed to knock the wind out of her sails and he seized the opportunity to dive in before she could bluster another refusal.

'Why not come along and have some fun? It's the perfect opportunity for you to meet the great and good of the sporting world. The after-show party can go on all night and there will be plenty of famous names there. I know, I won it a couple of years ago.'

Andy looked at him, wide eyed, as though he had just suggested running down the street wearing nothing but a cheeky grin and a pair of red stilettos.

'*Fun?* Perhaps it sounds like fun to you, but to me it is my worst possible nightmare.'

'Why? These celebrities are just people, the same as you and I.'

'Celebrities? That award ceremony has television crews, reporters and paparazzi six feet deep at the red carpet. If I went to an event like that I would be the wallflower who sneaks off to the kitchens to get some peace and quiet.'

Andy took a breath and shuddered for effect. 'Thank you for the invitation but that is not my kind of scene. *At all.* You can tell me all about it when you get back and I'll watch the highlights on TV. Have a nice time.'

'I intend to. But I didn't explain myself. You wouldn't be in the kitchens, and there is no way that you could ever be mistaken for a wallflower. Oh, no. I would never let you out of my sight for a second.'

Andy flung her arms out wide. 'You are still not listening. You need a glamorous sleek girl like that gorgeous blonde Jason was talking to just now.'

'Ah.' Miles nodded, his brow creased. 'The lovely Tiffany. Great girl, but unfortunately her talents did not extend to filing anything other than her nails and she cried when my dear brother asked her to coordinate the press for the award ceremony on Saturday night. *Actually cried.*'

'Stop it,' she said, trying not to laugh, and waggled her hands at him. 'I'm not sleek. I'm one of the ordinary girls who actually runs the place but from behind the scenes. Just the thought of those cameras pointing at me when I totter down a red carpet gives me palpitations.' And she gave a loud sigh and leant back on the balustrade, eyes closed.

'Andy,' he said in his best melted-chocolate voice, and as she half opened one eye he shuffled forwards, his gaze fixed on her face. And the look he was giving her was so absolutely carnivorous that she forgot to breathe.

'Don't let anyone tell you that you are ordinary. From what I have seen, you are one of the most extraordinary women I have ever met. And as for sleek?' His lips lifted into a smile that sent hot flames to warm the pit of her stomach. 'Sleek is much overrated in my opinion. I'm looking for more than sleek. I'm looking for real.'

Heat shimmered in the air and she could almost hear the clock chiming in the gallery in the cutting silence that separated her from Miles.

'Are we still talking about the date?' she finally murmured, his hot gaze still burning her face.

'What do you think?' he replied, biting his lip to suppress a smile.

Andy inhaled slowly, trying to make her brain work while Miles was looking at her like that and failing.

'I could use a girl who has no truck with this ridiculous game we all play called fame, but is polite enough not to tell someone that to their face. With a girl like that, I might be able to survive the night without socking someone or showing Jason up.'

His gaze slid up from her hands to her face, but his thumbs continued to stroke the back of her hand as he locked eyes with hers.

'That girl is you, Andy Davies. I choose you. Say yes and in return...I promise to do everything I can to help you with your career.'

She took a sharp intake of breath and her eyes flickered into life with that same fire he had seen back in the gallery.

'What do you mean? My career? You don't know anything about my career.'

Miles shrugged. 'Yes, I do. I know passion and

talent when I see it and, from what you've just told me, you have not had the opportunity to make your dream a reality until now. Those cards you have in that bag are only the start, Andy. Cory Sports uses professional designers who are always looking out for new talent. Talent like yours.'

'So now you are bribing me to be your date in exchange for helping me to find an outlet for my designs. Is that what you are saying?' Andy asked, with disbelief in her voice.

'Absolutely,' he replied with a single slow nod.

'You should be ashamed of yourself.'

'Not in the slightest. Because I am quite serious. Come out with me for one date. One. And I give you my word that I will do what I can to help your career. It's not often I have the chance to make a girl's dream come true. I rather like it. What do you say?'

She licked her lips and seemed to be working through the options.

It was now or never.

'One date.'

He nodded his head slowly up and down. 'One evening. And of course, as my date you should prepare yourself to be pampered with every luxury known to woman along the way. All part of the deal. No extra charge.'

Andy seemed to be biting on the inside of her lip, but then her shoulders dropped and she gave him a small, but warm half-smile.

'Pampering?' she replied, breaking the thick tense air that filled the few inches of space between them. 'Why didn't you say that in the first place? It has been a while since I had some pampering.'

'Then you will come with me? A week on Saturday. Eight till late?' Miles said as he leant forwards and kissed her forehead with the lightest possible touch of his lips, then her temple. 'Yes? Excellent,' he whispered in her ear before sliding away with a beaming grin. 'It is going to be quite a night.'

Then without warning he wrapped his arms around her slight body in a great bear hug, which seemed to force her air from her lungs, then stood back and rubbed his hands together.

'Right. Down to business,' he smouldered. 'You have taken time out of your life to show me those wonderful art works that make your heart sing. The very least I can do is offer to give you some idea of my passion in return. That way you'll have a fighting chance of keeping up with what we are talking about during the show.'

'I have to go surfing?' she gasped in disbelief.

'Not unless I can kidnap you and whisk you off to Tenerife. I was actually thinking of something a little closer to home. But I'll be in touch.'

And he lifted both of her hands to his lips and gave them one kiss before releasing her.

'We just have enough time to go through that pitch again before your meeting. Ready? Let's go and dazzle them,' he smirked, then grabbed her hand and took off, bad leg and all, dragging her behind him.

'I must be hearing things,' Jason said, peering at Miles over the top of his spectacles. 'For a moment there I thought you just said that you had to bribe the lovely Andy to go on a date after she turned you down. I'm shocked.'

'That would be correct,' Miles replied through bites of sandwich made from four slices of bread, half a pound of cheese, smothered in mayonnaise and several sliced tomatoes, which passed for a light snack. 'On the other hand, remind me again who you are taking to the most important event of our season? Um? Oh, yes, I remember now. Going solo. Again.'

Jason blew out long and low. 'True. But I am not the one who has been pacing the floor for the last hour and cannot sit still for more than ten minutes at a time—and, yes, I know your knee needs work, but please, just tell me that Andy is not just another form of distraction? Because I am the one staying in London who will have to pick up the pieces.'

'Distraction?' Miles sniffed. 'Maybe. Because talking to Andy certainly beats being cooped up in an airless office all day. But I meant what I told her. We have business skills and contacts she can use. And you can stop looking at me like that. One night. And that's it. No expectations on either side. Just how I like it.'

Jason looked at Miles through narrowed eyes. 'You have been whining on for months that you are not prepared to go solo in front of the other sportsmen and I get that. Truly. I do. You are back on your feet and you want the rest of the world to see you in your full glory with a lovely lady on your arm. All hail the great hero. But why am I getting the feeling that it is more than that?'

'Never mind the great hero part. We need to show the people who matter that the business is still in good hands. And I never asked you to set me up with some dates.'

'No, you didn't, because you have a problem asking anyone for help, even if they are your own family.'

Jason sat back in his computer chair and twirled it around to face Miles.

'Why are you going to this much trouble? Remember that fashion shoot we did in Bali last year? Those lovely ladies were all from the same London agency. I can pick up the phone to any one of ten girls who would be happy to be your date for the evening. Why don't you want to take the easy route this time? After all, it's only one night.'

Miles put down his sandwich, his appetite suddenly gone, and turned back from the open patio door. 'You really are clueless sometimes, do you know that? The last thing I need is another bikini model. Great girls, every one of them. But for this event I need someone different, and not in showbiz if I can help it. Andy is great. Quirky. I like her.'

Jason tapped his fingers on the edge of his chair as Miles glowered at him, then leant forwards and rested his elbows on his knees before asking in a low voice, 'Is this about Lori? Because I am happy to cover the meet and greet at the award ceremony if you are worried about seeing her again.'

'Worried?' Miles snorted as he pushed himself to his feet. 'Why should I be worried? Lori has already moved on to become the official girlfriend of one of the world's finest footballers. I am happy for her.'

'Happy,' Jason repeated. 'Oh, boy. I should have known. Here's an idea. Walk away. Why put yourself through the awkward moment when you see each other again for the first time since the accident? The latest range of surf gear is due to roll out at the trade fair in Honolulu next week. The manager would love for you to be there. Sun. Sea. Fun. And think of the publicity.'

'Not going to happen. I am fine. Professional and fine.'

Miles slapped his hand down hard on Jason's shoulder, making him wince. 'You worry too much. It's okay. Besides, I would much rather supervise the aqua-therapy programme this afternoon than squeeze myself behind a desk for any longer than I have to or into an aircraft seat. My knee won't take a long flight. Not yet.'

His hand suddenly stilled. 'Aqua therapy. I wonder...' And with a laugh he hobbled off to his room. 'I might just be able to persuade the lovely Andy to spend time with me after all. See you later and best of luck with the office systems.'

'Yes, fine. Go,' Jason sighed loudly and slapped his forehead. 'Don't worry about me. Just leave me to sort the mess out. I'll be okay. You go ahead and enjoy yourself.'

'No doubt about that,' Miles replied with a hand gesture. 'No doubt at all.'

'Charming. But aren't you forgetting something?'

Jason dived into his trouser pocket and pulled out a folded scrap of paper. 'I might have noted down the telephone number when Andy called this afternoon... She wanted to tell you that the museum have asked to see her complete range of greetings cards. Oh—didn't I mention that before? Silly me… Miles, what are you doing with that fork? Get off me!'

CHAPTER SEVEN

From: Andromeda@ConstellationOfficeServices
To: saffie@saffronthechef
Subject: What to do about the millionaire
I wish you would stop scolding me so much.
Blame Nigel if you like, but the last thing I want
or need right now is a dinner date where I won't
know what cutlery to use for what course, and I
am bound to say the wrong thing. He is just being
kind. That's all.

You know that I am clueless when it comes to
sport.

And no. I won't organise a double date for you,
me and the Gibson twins.

My life is already complicated enough.

Oh, must go—cards to paint.

Love ya, Andy the professional artist or something like that.

ANDY sat down at the worktop she was using as
her bedroom desk and stroked the thick paper

and lustrous colours of the print she had bought at the museum. This was where she was happiest. Alone with her illustrations. This was where she could most truly express what she was made of and what she did best.

Picking up the calligraphy pen she had been using for the lettering on one of her Christmas card designs, she carefully and slowly wrote his name in a round font, then italics, then gothic script.

Miles Gibson.

It was a strong name with two wonderful leading capitals.

A strong name for a strong man. A powerful man.

A smile crept up on her and she pressed her lips together tight.

Contrary. Unpredictable. Sporty. Domineering. And those were just his finer qualities. The list could go on.

Tempted? Oh, yes, she had been tempted.

Andy was so preoccupied with writing his name that when her mobile rang she picked it up without checking to see who the caller was, flipped it open, lifted it to her ear and said, 'Andy Davies.'

'Hey, girl,' a deep male voice said, and the pen she was holding dug into the paper, made a splodge of red ink and twisted the nib.

'Oh, rats,' she hissed, and tried to soak up the ink.

'I prefer hello,' Miles replied, his voice lifting up at the end in amusement.

'Oh, no, not you.' She frowned. 'I just spilt some ink, but it was only a test piece, nothing to worry about.'

She held the phone away from her mouth, rolled her eyes and grimaced. Was it possible to sound more stupid and pathetic?

She took a breath, smiled and tried to speak as though her brain was connected to the mouth. 'Back now. Shall we start again? Hello. What are you up to? And how did you find my number?'

He breathed out hot and fast. 'It turns out that my brother is a member of the gym at the hotel next door. And they have a hot tub. And Jason made a note of your number when you called today.'

Then his voice dropped several decibels and he half whispered in a tone that she could pour over ice cream, 'And how about you? What are you up to?'

'I'm at my desk painting stained-glass Christmas cards,' she murmured, her eyes closed so that she could listen to his voice without any visual distractions. 'Why do you ask?'

'I hear that the museum want to see your artwork,' he whispered. 'Congratulations. I would like to help you celebrate.'

It was a good thing she was sitting down, because suddenly all the wind went out of her sails.

'Thing is, if you are like me, you'll probably be working hard at making those pieces the best work you have ever done. And loving it. But you know what they say… All work and no play… So I have a suggestion. And don't panic. It is not another date. Our deal was strictly for a one-off event. Think of this as more of a research trip. And I know how much you love research.'

The bottom sank out of her stomach and she slapped the side of her head.

'Cory Sports sponsor an aqua-therapy pro-gramme at a couple of London swimming pools. We've just opened a new class and I'm going to head down to check on how it is doing. Want to come out and play?'

Andy stepped out of the taxi cab into the cool dusky air, and immediately tugged the belt of her navy raincoat a little tighter.

What was the dress code for meeting millionaire CEOs at swimming pools for a research trip? Research into how mad she was to agree to this in the first place. So what if his pitch had been brilliant and the shop loved her proposal. It was the artwork that had swung it, not just the clever marketing ploy.

Casual, Miles had said. What did that mean? Casual by her standards meant loose pants and sweatshirt and fluffy slippers. And Saffie had just laughed her head off when she rang her for advice. No help at all.

And where was she? The cab had dropped her off in front of a small shopping arcade in the middle of a residential area of Victorian and Edwardian houses with a sprinkling of modern flats and bungalows.

No flash glass and stone buildings here. No

photographers of paparazzi—just a sign pointing her towards a community gym and pool.

Two minutes later, Andy found her way to the ladies' changing room, drew open the door and instantly reeled back in surprise at the groups of lovely older ladies who were crammed around the lockers, all chatting and laughing and peering into bags and holdalls. But what really struck her was that, irrespective of their age, size and shape, every one of them was wearing a brightly coloured one-piece swimming costume that would not be out of place on some tropical beach. Huge red blossoms, birds of paradise and exotic butterflies clashed with huge banana leaves and gold ribbon trim and swim racer backs.

The room was a riot of colour and life and, try as she might, Andy could not help but laugh out loud in delight and astonishment.

This was the last thing she had expected to find in a small local gym in a residential area of London, but the colour scheme certainly matched the temperature. She had never been in a changing area that was this warm before. Tropical was about right.

'Hey, ladies—any of those swimming costumes left over? They're brilliant!'

'And they pull in the boys,' the nearest lady replied, which set the others off into an explosion of helpless giggling, which was probably not such a good idea for the lady in the wheelchair who had to gasp for breath because she was laughing so much.

Leaving them to their fun, Andy stowed her coat and boots and slipped her feet into a pair of non-slip pool shoes.

Time to find out where Miles had got to.

Andy drew back the swing doors and stepped out onto the tiles. Bright overhead lights reflected back from the water, the light broken by a swimmer doing strong front crawl, length after length. Andy looked up, just in time to see Miles Gibson hauling himself up over the edge of the pool.

Too proud to use the steps at the shallow end.

And the breath seemed to catch in her lungs as she ogled and kept on ogling.

Strong abs. Long muscular legs. Dark hairline going down to his trunks. Spectacular shoulders. She had not expected him to be so fit after months of hospital treatment. Or so gorgeous out of his clothes. Why was she always attracted to the muscular types? She had spent way too much time working in offices if this was what she was missing.

As she watched Miles shook his head back, showering water droplets down over his shoulders and the stunning rippling muscles across his wide back.

Her throat was dry, her palms clammy and walking and talking at the same time were going to be a challenge until he put some clothing on.

Miles Gibson was sex on legs.

Seriously.

Andy broke the spell by sighing in appreciation— way too loudly.

He smiled up at her as she calmly padded across to the poolside bench, but as she passed him his towel his face fell and he instantly dropped the towel over his lap and thighs.

'What? No bikini?' he asked, waggling his eyebrows.

'You should be so lucky,' she replied, 'but, speaking of swimwear, are you responsible for that collection of exotic birds that are waiting to explode out of the ladies' changing area?' She gestured with her head back towards the changing area. 'Because I have to tell you, it certainly brightened up my day.'

His reply was a slow nod and a lazy smile. 'Ladies' night. Cory Sports have spent the last two years developing a full programme of hot-water aqua-therapy classes. Their trainer is on the way but in the meantime the ladies have some fun and the company has some beta testing of its all-ages swimwear. Speaking of which—' and his brows tightened as his gaze scanned her body '—I thought you might have brought a swimming costume? Can't have all of the fun to myself.'

Andy sucked in a breath through her clenched teeth and focused her gaze on the wall murals.

'I was just admiring the pool. Such lovely colours. And warm too.'

'A nice ninety-five degrees. Great for arthritis and rheumatism and a whole raft of other conditions, such as sports injuries. And why are you avoiding my question?'

'I went to a private school which had its own pool. A cold-water swimming pool. The gym teacher thought that icy swimming classes were character forming and invigorating for the pupils.'

'Were they?'

'Of course not. I hated swimming lessons. We all did. I think it put most of us off swimming for life.'

Miles looked at her for a few seconds, his eyebrows high, before giving a small cough.

'Andy. Are you saying that...?'

She nodded. 'Can't swim. Scared of the water. Would you like another towel?'

Andy had only just finished speaking when the door to the changing room opened and an explosion of colour and laughter edged slowly out towards the steps at the shallow end of the pool.

'Scared of the water?' Miles replied, from behind her back. 'I've been teaching people to swim all of my life. That's why I worked this new programme into the schedule. Water confidence. It means working with the ladies one to one but it gets results.'

'Of course it does,' Andy said as she watched the ladies splash about in the warm water. 'Because you want to share your passion. And something tells me that you would be very good at that.' She turned back towards Miles, but took one step too far, colliding with his shoulder, sending his leg slipping on the moist slick floor.

She felt herself falling sideways with him, out of control, just waiting for the crunch as she hit the floor.

Only she didn't hit anything.

Two hands grabbed her waist, and as she moved to push herself back up, his right hand moved instinctively to give her more support. And slid under her loose sweater onto her bare skin.

The effect was electrifying. In a second she was upright, one hand pressed against the muscles of his bare chest, her forehead in contact with his chin and neck, as he pressed her to his body so he could take her weight. She felt the raised stubble on the side of his face, a faint tang of a citrus aftershave and swimming-pool antiseptic and something else. Something essentially masculine. That combination of sweat, tension and musky personal aroma, which was driving cave girls wild thousands of years ago, and was working just fine right now.

She closed her eyes and revelled in the sensation as his hand moved just a few centimetres higher on the skin at her waist. She wanted him to go higher, a lot higher.

Oh, God, this felt so right. So very right.

Neither of them spoke as she pressed herself into his neck, only too aware that his breathing was matching her own heart rate. Racing. Only she had stopped breathing, and her single breath broke the moment. Both of his hands lifted at the same time as she opened her eyes and pushed gently from his body.

And took three steps back, creating some space between them.

It had been a mistake coming here. Seeing Miles like this. A really bad mistake.

Because every cell in her body was screaming for her to give into this attraction and do something mad, like jump onto his lap and kiss him breathless. And where would that leave her?

Nowhere. Alone and discarded. And wouldn't that feel good?

The whole incident had only taken a few seconds but she didn't have the guts to look at him when she eventually spoke.

'That was embarrassing. I almost needed your lifeguarding skills there for a moment.'

'Are you okay?'

His voice was low, caring. Almost whispered. He was breathing as heavily as she was. Andy fought to put together a coherent response. 'I'm fine. Thank you.'

But when Miles stepped forwards, he staggered back slightly and tried to massage his calf muscles into working, but then his knee seized up completely and he had to lean against the bench to relieve the pressure, wincing in pain.

'Cramp?' Andy asked.

'Not exactly,' Miles replied with a sarcastic shrug, then smiled and dropped his shoulders with the gentlest of touches on her arm. 'Sorry. I sometimes forget that the rest of the world doesn't have much interest in my surfing career.'

'Ah, I don't usually read the sports section of the newspaper. But I should imagine that professional sportsmen have a lot of injuries to cope with.' She glanced down at his leg. 'Does it hurt?'

'More than Jason knows. And the painkillers knock me out. So I put up with it.'

He sniffed and hobbled over to the bench. 'And you're right, when you are pushing yourself to the limit, you do get injured. Which makes this—'

and he scrubbed even harder at his leg '—even harder to tolerate, because I didn't fall off a board. I got hit by a truck.'

Her jaw dropped. 'Of course. You mentioned it at the museum. How did it happen?'

'I was in a small sports car. It was raining and the truck driver was so drunk he could hardly stand,' he snorted. 'I remember walking out of my girlfriend's beach house on Tenerife into the rain with not a care in the world. And twenty-four hours later I woke up in a city hospital and most of my body was broken.'

Miles stretched out his leg, and began massaging the sinewy calf muscles. 'I was too doped up on painkillers and sedatives to take much in at the time but I recall flashes of my dad's face and people in white coats and words like fractures. Pierced lungs. Hip replacement. Pins. Then they knocked me out again so they could do what they had to do.'

She gasped and stopped breathing for a second. 'What about the other driver—were they…?'

'Cuts and bruises. The drunk was lucky. I wasn't.'

Andy exhaled slowly and blinked at him. 'How did you get through it?'

'I didn't. Good thing my parents understood that yelling at them was only a temporary phase. They were just pleased that I had survived.'

'But you did it. You came out in one piece,' Andy whispered and looked at him.

'Several pieces. And you can still see the joins.'

Andy could not help it. She stared at the puckered red and white skin for several seconds. The scars ran from knee to upper thigh and she could see where the incisions and pins had been, but it was not gory or scary.

It was simply his leg.

'Nice scars.' She nodded, her lips pressed together.

He blinked, looked at his knee, then back at her face. 'Nice scars? Is that it? The girls love my scars. I thought that at the very least you would be impressed and leap into my arms because I am a wounded hero.'

'Over a few leg scars? Please,' she replied in a nonchalant and relaxed voice. 'But your family must have been scared for you.'

'Damn right.'

'Does it affect your swimming?' Andy asked in a completely natural voice with a smile on her lips. Oblivious to the knife she had just slipped up into his heart.

Miles froze, his gaze scanning her face, but saw only genuine concern staring back at him. Not disgust that he was broken and useless, or pity for what his body had been like.

'Not in classes like this, no.'

She sniffed and nodded. 'Good, because, I have to tell you, those ladies are a real handful. You are going to need all of your expert coaching skills to keep the girls in check today.'

Coaching skills?

Miles coughed. And then stilled. She had a point. He had always loved teaching, no matter what age the beginners were. He could do that. Leg or no leg.

The old light switched back on inside him, warmed by the grin on Andy's face as she waved at the ladies.

Time to complete his side of their bargain. 'Speaking of families. Would you like to come back to the Cory Sports building this evening and meet some of my team? Jason is in the mood to cook and he loves having people around. It would be nice to help you celebrate your success at the museum.'

'You want me to come to your apartment?'

Andy's heart was pounding. She would be alone in an apartment with two single men she had only just met. Now that was more than a little scary.

Miles must have heard her thoughts because his next words were, 'Jason's apartment. And don't be scared. My brother has many skills and cooking is one of them. I left him in the kitchen peeling oranges. I think this is a good sign. Plus I've already mentioned your artwork to our website designer, Peter. He'll be there with his wife, Lisa, tonight so there is at least one more creative person in the room. And then there is your umbrella. A sad case. It is missing you terribly.'

He paused and exhaled slowly. 'So what shall I tell Jason? Does he set another place at the table?'

'One question. Would I have to do the washing up?'

She heard him chuckle, deep and resonant, and the rich sound filled her head.

'No. All taken care of. Your job will be to enjoy

yourself. Prepare to be positively pampered. I'll even come along and pick you up if you like.'

'Well, in that case, I would be delighted to eat home-cooked food. Thank you. But it would be easier if I took a cab to your office.'

'You got it. Oh—and, Andy.'

'Yes?'

'Just so that you know. I would never stand you up. Never.'

And with that he pushed himself to his feet and strolled over to the cluster of ladies at the shallow end of the pool, who instantly mobbed him like fan girls meeting a pop star. Twenty seconds later they were all laughing like teenagers and splashing in the warm water. Having the time of their lives.

And all the time Andy was sitting on the bench, watching him in the water. Just watching him.

From: Andromeda@ConstellationOfficeServices
To: saffie@saffronthechef
Subject: Dinner with the Gibson Twins
Saffie, you are terrible. Jason might be an excellent cook.

Of course I know that they are millionaires and

probably have their food pre-prepared by chefs and supplied in posh microwave dishes, but Miles did say that cooking is Jason's hobby. And, yes, I shall give you a full report of what we ate and how it tasted. And, no, I will not take photographs of the penthouse or the food. Unless I really have to, because otherwise you wouldn't believe me.

This means I am bound to show myself up.

Thanks again for the loan of your posh cashmere.

Wish me luck

Andy the terrified.

'More cheese, Andy? I tried to save you the last slice of the quince membrillo but I was too late— the amazing eating machine here got to it first.'

Jason gestured with the cheese knife towards Miles, who threw his hands up into the air in protest. 'Hey—can I help it if I have a healthy appetite? Anyway, you're one to talk. I only turned my back for two minutes to help Lisa on with her coat and what was left of those fancy chocolates Peter brought had done a magic disappearing act.'

Jason sniffed and flung his head with a dramatic twist. 'Cook's perks.' He pressed his hand to his chest. 'Sweet tooth. I confess. Happy now?' And dodged the napkin that Miles threw at him.

Andy laughed and sat back on the lovely cream leather sofa and patted her stomach. 'Thanks, but I couldn't eat another thing. And don't forget—I have to have that recipe for the pork with ginger and orange. It was the most delicious thing I have ever eaten.'

Jason abandoned his tray and lifted Andy's hand and kissed the back of her knuckles. 'Praise indeed. Thank you, kind lady.' Then he peered at Miles with narrowed eyes. 'See. Did you hear that? Everybody else liked my cooking. According to Peter my menu was inspired… Beat that if you can. Seeing as you can barely use a kettle.'

'Champagne sorbet? Please. That's way too girly. I was expecting at least a chocolate tart or one of those creamy cake things.'

'Don't listen to a word Miles says,' Andy tutted and smiled up at Jason. 'It was a wonderful meal and I feel positively pampered. And very guilty. Are you sure I can't help you with the washing up?'

Jason gestured for her to sit back down with both hands palm down. 'Dishwashers. Marvellous things. You just sit back and relax and try the coffee while this one keeps you company—if you can stand it.'

Then in a flash he had loaded up a tray with the flatware and was off behind the marble slab that separated the kitchen from the dining area of the huge open-plan apartment.

Andy indulged in a secret snigger and raised the tiny espresso cup to her nose and inhaled deeply.

'Oh, that is so wonderful. I love good coffee.'

'Here. Allow me.' Miles got up from the dining table so that he could top up her cup with the fragrant piping-hot brew. 'Jase knows the grower in the West Indies. There are a few specialist shops in London who import the beans but he insists on grinding them to his own specification every time. It takes longer but that's my brother for you. Things have to be just right or it bothers him like mad.'

There was a real sense of pride in that voice, which to Andy sounded as mellow and rich as the chocolate notes in the coffee.

'I noticed. He was so worried that Peter and Liz were going to be late for their babysitter that he sent the limo for them. But of course, I blame you completely for keeping them laughing so late in the evening.'

Miles pointed to the chest of his navy V-necked designer jumper and faked an expression of total innocence. '*Moi?* I cannot think what you could mean.'

'Really?' Andy picked up one of the photo albums from the coffee table. 'So those photos of Peter and Jason hanging off the rigging of an old sailing ship dressed up as pirates just happened to be lying around. Hmm?'

Miles sniggered. 'It took me days to find a parrot which was docile enough to sit on Peter's shoulder. Shame that my mother had fed the poor bird to bursting and not bothered to tell us before we took her out on open water.'

He closed his eyes and sniggered. 'Classic.'

'You were very cruel. I liked Peter. And he was so kind about the party invitation I painted for Elise.'

'No, he wasn't.' Miles shook his head, then sat down on the hard chair facing Andy with his long legs stretched out in front of him. 'Peter does not do kind. He meant it.'

Miles saluted Andy with his water glass. 'He

loved your work. It's as simple as that. You have to remember that Peter helped to design the Cory Sports logo based on the Corazon heart theme that you picked up on. It was a genius idea to take the letter C and work in the hearts and Spanish flowers in blue and gold. Genius. And that is not a word that gets used around here very often.'

Miles dug down into his trouser pocket and passed a business card across the coffee table to Andy, who stared at it for a few seconds before picking it up.

'When Peter LeBlanc asks you to call him about buying the exclusive rights to your design—he has already made up his mind. These are his contact details. Have a think about how much you want to charge, then give him a call. He'll be expecting you. And tomorrow would be good.'

Andy opened her mouth to reply, looked down at the card, which she could barely read because her eyes were blurred with tears, then put it on the table and exhaled slowly.

'Tomorrow? This is all a bit fast for me, Miles.'

'We recognise quality workmanship when we see it, Andy. You are a very talented artist and we would like to buy one of your designs. Is that a problem? Aren't you interested in that type of painting any longer?'

'Interested? This is my dream project. I love the illuminated artwork. No—it's not the work. It's me. I am not used to people taking me seriously as an artist. And it has come as rather a shock. First the museum wants to sell my Christmas card designs and now Peter wants to talk to me about the logo. This has been a very overwhelming week.'

She pressed her finger to her nose and blinked away a sniffle. 'I know that I must sound like a total idiot, but I have been working for a long time to get my artwork off the ground and now everything has come all at once and my poor head is having a hard time coping with the idea that someone has confidence in my work. I am far more used to being ridiculed about my so-called foolish hobby. Sorry.'

Miles sat back in silence, locked his hands behind his head and stretched out his long, long legs so that the muscles in his thighs stretched the fine fabric until it was taut. The expression on his face as he looked at her was so intense that Andy started chewing on her lower lip and shuffling on the slippery leather, her relaxed and happy mood a thing of the past.

She felt that he was weighing her up. Judging her.

It was Miles who broke the tension by flicking through one of the photo albums until he came to a full-page print of the young Miles standing on an upturned plastic crate, grinning from ear to ear at the person holding the camera.

Clutched in his hands was a tiny silver-coloured trophy and he was holding it aloft like an Olympic athlete. Standing on one side of him was a bare-chested Jason in board shorts and, on the other, an older man who looked so much like Miles and Jason that it could only be their father. They had their arms wrapped around Miles's shoulders and their joy leapt out of the photograph and brought a smile to Andy's face.

'I was seventeen. I had just won the Best of Cornwall surfing championship, the sun was shining and I thought life could not get any better. My mother took the photograph, then we walked back along the beach and stopped for fish and chips. And that was when they told me that they were selling everything and moving to Tenerife so that I could train as a professional surfer.'

Miles closed the album with a snap. 'They gave me a chance to show what I could do. And I was so scared that I would let them down, it paralysed me. But I took the risk. And I have never regretted it.'

His gaze dropped to her hands, and he gently turned her right hand over and ran his fingertip along the palm, only too aware that her body seemed to shiver at his touch, and not just from the cold night air.

'You have a long life line. Same as me.'

Then he inhaled slowly and curled her fingers over her palm and held them there.

'Take the chance, Andy. Show us what you are made of. Show us what you can do.'

She hesitated, her breathing fast and hot.

'Is that what you are doing, Miles? Showing everyone what you are made of? It must be hard trying to prove that, even after your accident, you still have the same joy in your work that you had when you were seventeen.'

Miles froze.

The same joy? No. He could never go back to

being that same happy teenager with so much to look forward to and so little clue about how much work it was going to take to become the world champion. And stay there.

The seventeen-years-old Miles had been bursting with power and potential and the sheer joy in his sport.

Joy. When was the last time he had truly found joy in what he was doing? Adrenaline rush—yes. Excitement and exhilaration, every time. But joy? No, he had not felt true joy for years. Even before the accident his life had become an endless battle to stay on top of his fitness and competitions and business work.

Little wonder he'd had no time to realise that his so-called girlfriend was more interested in the celebrity circuit than spending time with him.

A dark cloud called disappointment and frustration passed over his heart and he sat back hard in his chair.

When had he lost his joy in the sport?

Miles inhaled slowly, only too aware that Andy was still looking at him, waiting for his reply.

She smiled at him as though she could read his mind, and the warmth of that smile seemed to penetrate his thick skull and blow away the dark clouds, leaving a calm blue-sky day behind.

Strange. He had never thought about it that way until now.

And yet this girl had seen it in him. How did she do that? How did she get under his skin?

An old familiar yearning started deep in his belly and wound its way to other parts of his anatomy.

Attraction. And more.

After Lori he had promised himself that he would stick to casual relationships.

But maybe the cost was too high a price to pay? What happened if he met someone who was more interested in him rather than his celebrity status? How was he going to handle that and risk being rejected again?

Miles straightened his back.

This was one time he was going to walk away from the danger.

He didn't need this. Not now. He could fight it. He had to. Anything else would be too complicated and way too dangerous for both of them.

All he needed was a stand-in date for Saturday night and then he would be out of here and things would be back to normal. That was what he had to focus on.

Whether he wanted it that way or not.

It was Andy who broke the silence.

'Some of us have changed direction so many times I think I am going around in circles most days. Do you ever feel like trying something new?'

He replied with a dismissive snort. 'Never. Cory Sports needs Miles Gibson to be standing on some podium somewhere—the champion kite surfer. King of the surf. That's my job. And I happen to be very good at it.'

'And now you can add expert swimming coach and business mentor to the list. It is a good thing that you are so modest,' Andy replied, and reached for her coffee cup, her eyes not leaving his.

And just like that the air between them bristled with static electricity. It bounced back and forwards, sparking all the way as the silence filled the room. The subtle Spanish background music was gone. Replaced by the sound of their breathing. And the hot crackle of the tension as their eyes locked and stayed locked.

Miles leant forwards so that his whole body was focused on her, eyes bright and smiling.

'Will you at least think about it? Then call Peter when you are ready.'

Then he pushed himself slowly to his feet before she could reply, and was at her side, wrapping his down coat around her shoulders with a low chortle and sliding open the floor-to-ceiling glass patio doors. 'Let's get some air.'

CHAPTER EIGHT

ANDY stepped out onto a long tiled terrace, and what she saw in front of her took her breath away.

The light showers of rain had cleared to leave a star-kissed cool evening. And stretched out, in every direction, was London. Her city. Dressed and lit and bright and shiny and sparking with Christmas decorations and the lights from homes and streets.

It was like something from a movie or a wonderful painting. A moment so special that Andy knew instinctively that she would never forget it.

She grasped hold of the railing and looked out over the city, her heart soaring, all doubt forgotten in the exuberant joy of the view.

It was almost a shock to feel a warm arm wrap the coat closer around her shoulders and she turned sideways to face Miles with a grin and clutched onto the sleeve of his sweater.

'Have you seen this? It's astonishing. I thought

the view from the gallery at the museum was spectacular, but this is wonderful. I love it.'

'I know. I can see it on your face.'

Then he turned forwards and came to stand next to her on the balcony, his left hand just touching the outstretched fingers of her right.

'You probably don't realise it, but there are very few people who are totally honest and open about their feelings. But you are one of them. You have a special gift, Andromeda Davies. You aren't afraid to tell people the truth about how you feel. And I envy you that.'

'You. Envy me? What do you mean?' Andy asked, taken aback by the tone in his voice. For the first time since they met, Miles sounded hesitant and unsure, in total contrast to the man who had been gibing with his brother and friends.

'Honesty can make you vulnerable.'

Miles looked down at Andy's fingers and his gaze seemed to lock onto how his fingers could mesh with hers so completely. 'This last year has taught me a few things. There are some things in life you can control, Andy. Some you can't. But I know one thing. I am done with long-term planning. That is out of the window and gone.

Because you don't know what is coming your way. You can't. So live for the day. Take the opportunities that come along and enjoy them while you can. That's my new motto.'

Andy looked into his face and remembered to breathe again.

'And how is that working for you?' She smiled.

'Actually not too badly. It means that instead of riding the waves in South America I am here in London enjoying time out with my brother and a lovely lady.'

He held one of Andy's hands. 'I have even found the time to go on an Internet date. Imagine that.'

'Yes. Imagine. Did I say brave earlier? Maybe madcap might be a better expression. I don't have any sports injuries or scars and bruises like that, Miles. Scar-free learning. That's my motto. Maybe that is why I am even more scared than usual. I need that forward planning to make sense of my life and make sure that the bills get paid.'

'No scars and bruises? Yes, you have, you have plenty of scars.'

He pressed two fingers flat onto her chest so they rested above her heart and she could feel the warm pressure of his fingertips through the fine cashmere wool. 'But they are not on the surface like mine are. They are all in here. And they hurt just as bad. Because I think other people pushed you beyond the limit of what you were ready to handle. But here is the thing. When you are competing against the world's best athletes, you soon learn that the only way you can win is to strive to reach your own limits of what you are capable of—not the limits anyone sets.'

'How do you know? What your limits are?'

'You don't. The only way to find out is by testing yourself. You would be astounded at what you are capable of. And if you don't succeed you learn from your mistakes and do what you have to do to get back up and try again until you can prove to yourself that you can do it. And then you keep on doing that over and over again.'

'No matter how many times you fall down and hurt yourself?'

'That's right. You've got it.'

Andy turned slightly away from Miles and looked out towards the horizon, suddenly needing to get some distance, some air between them. What he was describing was so hard, so difficult and so familiar. He could never know how many times she had forced herself to smile after someone let her down, or when she had been ridiculed or humiliated.

Andy blinked back tears and pulled the collar of the warm coat up around her ears while she fought to gain control of her voice. 'Some of us lesser mortals have been knocked down so many times that it is hard to bounce back up again, Miles. Very hard.'

His response was to reach out for her with both of his long strong arms and draw her into his chest so that her head rested on his shoulder. The warmth of his body encased her in a cocoon of strength and warm cashmere and she was content to cling onto him for a few seconds while the air seeped back into her lungs. Air that smelt of Miles and coffee and biscuits and frost and winter in the city.

'What is it, Andy?' he asked, his mouth somewhere in the vicinity of her hair. 'What does your heart yearn to do and you haven't gone there yet?'

'Me? Oh, I had such great plans when I was a teenager and the whole world seemed to be an open door to whatever I wanted. But then hard reality hit. Six months ago I was working three jobs and most evenings and weekends. Right now I have to think about whether I want to go back to a full-time day job working with men like Nigel, or try and earn enough from my artwork.'

She looked up into his smiling face but stayed inside the warm circle of his arms. 'Nigel is the ex-boyfriend I talked about. Or at least I thought he was my boyfriend. He worked in the same office with those girls you saw in the coffee shop the other evening. There was a lot of competition for clients, so when he asked me to help him work on a major new proposal I was pleased to help.'

Andy smoothed the fine fabric of his sweater as she spoke. 'He played every trick in the book to get me to work for nothing, night after night. The occasional pizza meal out. Drinks. Always promising that we could be a proper couple when the project was approved. Always teasing and telling me how important I was to him.'

Her hands stilled. 'He dumped me the day he got the client account.'

Tears pricked her eyes and she swallowed down the pain to get the words out. 'But do you know the worst part? The girls in the office knew that he was living with the CEO's daughter and that he was just using me to get the work done so he could pass it off as his own. And they didn't tell me. They were having too much fun laughing behind my back. Have you any idea how humiliating that was? I couldn't...' She took a few sharp short breaths before going on. 'I couldn't work there a minute longer. I just couldn't. Do you understand?'

Miles replied by wrapping his long arms around her body in a warm embrace so tender that Andy surrendered to a moment of joy and pressed her head against his chest, inhaling his delicious scent as her body shared his warmth.

His hands made lazy circles on her back in silence for a few minutes until he spoke, the words reverberating inside his chest into her head. 'Better than you think. What did you do then?'

Andy shuffled back from him, laughed in a choked voice and then pressed both hands against his chest as she replied in a broken smile. 'Then I met up with Elise—and, well, you know the rest. I needed that part-time office job until the artwork takes off. Only now it looks like I need to organise myself if I want to sell my designs to you and the museum.'

He grabbed both of her arms as she tried to

slip away and looked at her straight in the eyes. 'I agree. Not nearly ambitious enough. Let's start again. And think big. Then bigger. It sounds so good I don't know why you haven't gone into design full-time before now.'

He tilted his head sideways to look at Andy as she moistened her lips, her mouth a straight line.

'Isn't it obvious?' she whispered after several long seconds. 'I'm too scared.'

'Scared of what? Failure? Hell, Jason and I made so many mistakes those first two years we must have been the laughing stock of the business. Good thing we were able to laugh at ourselves and enjoy the journey.'

'How did you do that? How did you laugh when you knew that you had taken a horrible decision which was going to cost you time and money? Because I don't know how to do that.'

'How? Because we felt like we were explorers, charting unknown territory, where every day was a new challenge.' Miles grinned, his face energised, the laughter lines hard in the artificial light flooding out from the dining room. Then he shrugged. 'And we had our parents behind us. Family all the way.'

'Family?' Andy repeated. 'Then you truly were lucky. Because all my family did was to ridicule me and everything I liked to do. I am on my own, Miles. Completely on my own. Can you understand that?'

Miles stood in silence, his gaze locked onto Andy's wide green eyes as she took in a few breaths of the cool night air.

Completely on her own? How was that possible? The hairs on the back of his neck flickered into life at the very thought of being without Jason and his parents and their circle of friends back on Tenerife, and he rubbed his hand over his neck to quieten them down.

They had been his lifeline, his strength and his back-up when times were hard as well as good.

The only people he would accept help from. *Ever.*

'No. I can't imagine being without my parents and family.'

He stepped forward one step and rubbed his hands up and down Andy's arms.

She flashed him a glance intended to make him back off but he ignored it anyhow.

'You talked about your parents at the museum. Have they, er...'

Andy rolled her eyes towards the balcony above their heads. 'Oh, still very much alive. Still mad as a bag of frogs and still trying to teach English in India. From the letters which turn up every few months they seem to be lurching from crisis to crisis with the occasional frantic phone call in the middle of the night pleading the need for emergency funds to pay for a new roof or replacement parts for some car or other. Practical household skills were not part of the private education in those days. My dad was one of those men who employed tradesmen to wire a plug. Do you get the picture?'

Miles sucked in air through his teeth. 'No. Not really. India. Wow.'

She shook her head and pointed to the balcony. 'I look at this city that I love and think of all of the opportunity that is out there and I fill up with excitement and enthusiasm and I want to do this so badly—and then I think about all of the unknowns and costs and pitfalls and I freeze. And put the plan back in the drawer to think about later.'

'Only there won't be a later. Will there? I am beginning to understand. And I don't blame you for taking the safer option.'

'Do not judge me. We aren't all sporting heroes!'

'I don't expect you to be,' Miles replied, and raised both hands in the air in submission. 'And I'm the last person on this planet who has the right to judge anybody. Don't forget—I have been there and I had my brother and family along for the ride and we still had to work like crazy to get our business started. A one-woman show is going to find it a lot tougher. You need time and money to get your art business off the ground.'

Andy glared at him, narrow lipped, her gaze scanning his face for a few seconds before her shoulders dropped and she sighed out loud. 'I know. And that has always been the problem. But I am sorry for snapping at you. This has been a tough week.'

'No problem. How about a suggestion instead? I know a couple of venture capital guys who have money to invest in new business ideas. All I have to do is make a few phone calls and…what? What now?'

'I don't want to carry any debt. No maxed-out

credit cards. No business loans, no venture capital investment. That's how my dad got into so much trouble and there is no way that I am going there. So thank you but no. I might be hard up but I have made some rules for myself.'

Miles inhaled very slowly and watched Andy struggle with her thoughts, her dilemma played out in the tension on her face.

She was as proud as anyone he had ever met. Including himself. Which was quite something.

And just like that the connection he had sensed between them from the moment he had laid eyes on her in that coffee shop kicked up a couple of notches. And the longer he watched her, the stronger that connection became, until he almost felt that it was a practical thing. A wire. Pulling them closer together.

And every warning bell in his body started screaming *Danger* so loudly that in the end he could not ignore it any longer. And this time he was the one who broke the wire and pulled away from her.

She shivered in the cool air, fracturing the moment, and he stepped back and opened the patio doors and guided her inside. And into the luxurious warmth of the apartment.

'No debt,' Miles murmured as he slipped his coat from her shoulders and gestured for her to get comfy on the sofa. 'That's a tough one. Well, you know how much I like a challenge.'

Then his eyes narrowed and a broad smile cracked his mouth. 'Here is an idea which won't cost you a penny but could be just what you need to get the business up and running.'

He moved onto the back of the sofa and grabbed hold of both of her shoulders so that she could not move an inch as he leant forwards until their noses were almost touching, his eyes locked onto hers.

'You like facts. Here are two. Jason asked me to come over to the London office for a few days so that we can work on the plan for the next product launch. And I didn't argue because my brother is a genius—but you must never tell him I said that.'

Andy took a breath but Miles got there first. 'No talking. But as it happens, I might have an hour or two to spare between physio sessions and meetings.'

Then he relaxed his grip a little and smiled. 'I thought about what you said at the pool today.

And you might have a point. I enjoy training. So… how would you like some help with that business plan? A website. Promotions. Marketing. All the things you need to get your artwork out for the world to see.'

She looked back at him, wide eyed. 'Would I have to wear a swimming costume?'

A great wide-mouthed grin illuminated his face as his gaze scanned her body from the heels of her boots to her hair clip, bringing that sparkle back into his eyes. 'Perhaps not. Way too distracting. So. What do you say? Can you spare an hour a day to get some business advice?'

From: Andromeda@ConstellationOfficeServices
To: Saffie@Saffronthechef
Hope your Saturday evening dinner service goes more smoothly this week.

Thanks again for your offer of your best designer dress and full kit. And you were right—the red works and there may well be some seriously high-class slutty photos.

Problem is. I am having kittens here. What am I going to do, Saffie? Help!

There are going to be TV cameras and photographers there tonight.

Miles is determined to introduce me to half the room as an illustrator. He has no clue that the first time I mention illuminated fifteenth-century bibles his posh guests will run off screaming or think I am high on hallucinogens.

The last thing I want to do is show him up in any way.

Maybe I can fake the flu? Or chicken pox? That might work. Top athletes hate disease.

Talk again in the morning. If I make it that far. Andy

Andy paced up and down on the bedroom carpet, her hands on her hips, as she moved from her bed to the wardrobe, then back to the bottom of her bed again.

The wardrobe door was open and she blinked at the contents for several minutes before striding purposefully forwards in Saffie's favourite red high-heeled sandals. Her hand stretched out to lift the red chiffon cocktail dress from the hanger, then froze and dropped away. Again.

Her shoulders slumped and she rested her

forehead on the waxed oak panel, not caring that she was ruining the make-up that had taken her an hour to put on, wipe off, then put on again in a different way.

Terrified that she was sending out the wrong message. Or was it the right message?

She had been aiming for elegant and attractive, while the girl who stared back at her from the mirror looked more like someone from a low-class burlesque show. Never mind the high-class slutty. She was the low-class slutty.

Reminder to self: find a job with a firm of hairdressers. Or beauticians. Or both.

This wasn't working.

She had been mad to even think that she was ready to go out on a date, with Miles Gibson, millionaire joint owner of Cory Sports. Even if it was for only one evening.

Andy tottered to her bed, fell backwards and let her arms dangle over the sides.

Had what happened with Nigel not taught her anything?

What if she had been right the first time and Miles was a chancer, and she was just about to make herself a laughing stock in exchange for a hot dinner and if she was lucky a glass of the house red?

Andy sniffed. No. That was unfair. Miles was not a cheapskate. He was a very successful businessman and professional sportsman. It would be a very nice dinner in a luxury hotel restaurant owned by one of those chefs who seemed to be on every television channel.

A restaurant where everyone would know that he was a multimillionaire slumming it with the girl who delivered party invitations. And she was fine with that. Better than fine. This was her life and she wasn't ashamed. Far from it.

What she was afraid of was being laughed at. Laughed and scoffed at because she had stepped outside her narrow circle and trusted someone not to use her.

Andy bit down on her inner lip. Deep inside in that secret place where she kept her dreams and most sacred wishes, she wanted to stride into that hotel in these red shoes as the equal of any of the other guests, including Miles. Strong and confident. Like the girl she used to be before life stomped on her confidence and squeezed it out like toothpaste from a tube.

Dratted Miles for reminding her about her other life.

Andy closed her eyes, her throat burning and tears stinging at the sides of her eyes.

She was pathetic.

This amazing, handsome and attentive man had chosen her to be his date for the evening. Which was so amazing that she still couldn't believe it.

Not that she had much time to prepare herself for the big night.

The past few days had passed in a blur of activity and mad work. Miles had not been kidding about how restless he was, but his pacing had slowly got better. He had kept his word and after a few hours going through the Cory Sports systems she had actually started to believe that she had the tools she needed to be a self-employed artist. Peter had set up meetings with their advertising company for next week so she had plenty to think about. But she had done it. She had taken the first baby steps.

And right there, every step of the way, had been Miles.

He had sat on the couch in Reception with his leg on the coffee table holding meetings with suppliers and giving interviews over the tele-phone—and all the time giving her furtive glances and the kind of not very discreet smiles that made Jason tut and dive back into his office to work on production plans so complex that Andy had taken one glance and left him to it.

So most of the time it had just been the two of them out front. Handling telephone calls and laughing about some newspaper article or sports magazine press clipping over the excellent coffee Jason insisted on making for her. And all the while Miles told her anecdotes about his work and past achievements and how this manufacturer or clothing outlet came to stock their clothing.

Strange how many times a day he found a way to brush against her hand with his, or look over her shoulder at some suddenly vital piece of information on the PC monitor. She had to stop the tickling, of course—that got completely out of hand and she had to scold him about being professional.

A smirk of supressed laughter flicked across Andy's face.

If this was business coaching then she was all for it.

And maybe it was just as well that she had been kept busy. It had kept her mind away from mulling over all of those intimate moments they had shared since he had walked into that coffee shop. His kisses and touch. His kindness. His quiet compassion. His humour.

A girl could fall for a man like that.

Hell. She was already halfway there.

Then her smile faded. But this evening was more than work—this was about Miles. She would never forgive herself if she messed up the most important event since his accident. And she only had an hour before facing the cameras.

Andy groaned and was just reaching for a pillow to pull over her head when her mobile phone rang on her bedside table.

She stretched out and flipped it open, but stayed lying down.

'Andy Davies.'

'Hey, Andy,' came a voice as smooth and delicious as dark mocha chocolate. 'My folks are having a beach barbecue tonight. I am thinking of making my excuses and jumping on the next flight to Tenerife. Want to elope with me?'

Tenerife? Flight? Elope?

Yes, please. I can be packed and ready in twenty minutes flat.

Deep breath.

'What?' She laughed. 'And miss a chance to hear all of the latest showbiz gossip from Saffie's favourite movie actor firsthand? Perish the thought.'

Andy started fiddling with a strand of hair one handed. 'I never took you for a quitter, Mr Gibson,' she replied with a laugh in her voice. 'Surely you are not going to allow a few reporters to thwart your plans for world domination?'

A manly cough was followed by a low growl and Andy imagined him glowering at the mobile phone. 'You know me so well, Miss Davies. Perhaps I should come over to your place now and you can talk me out of doing a runner?'

'Sorry. No can do. I am nowhere near ready. And I don't want to open the door in my underwear and dressing gown.'

The microsecond the words left her lips Andy winced. Wrong thing to say. *In so many ways.*

'Actually that would probably be the highlight of the evening. I could award points on the amount of lingerie on display and deduct points from the amount of Andy concealed. Sounds like a challenge.'

'And one you will never know,' she added hastily, desperate to change the subject. 'How is Jason's speech getting on?'

'Who? Never heard of him. Now back to this lingerie. Are you at home?'

'Might be,' she replied, not wanting him to have the satisfaction of knowing that she was lying on her bed in her underwear. And the red heels she needed to break in so that she would not fall flat on her face in front of the VIPs. 'Are you?'

'No. I'm still at Jason's place. As you well know. But I have this terrible problem. What to wear? I wonder if you could give me guidance on the matter.'

'Fashion advice? I am a little rusty on gentle-man's couture, but I can try. What are you wearing right now?'

She heard his breath catch, and then slapped her hand to her forehead. 'I meant…what suit are you wearing right now?'

'Of course you did,' he growled. 'I am actually sitting on my bed looking at the three suits I brought with me. But to answer your question?'

Andy pressed the phone to her ear and held her breath.

'Black boxers. Black socks. A knee brace so I can stand for a couple of hours without falling over. The aftershave our Paris perfumers have been working on for Cory but we haven't launched yet. Oh—and a smile. Because I am talking to you.'

Andy bit down on her lower lip as she had a vision of Miles wearing only boxers and socks and the room became remarkably warm all of a sudden. *Stay focused. Stay focused.*

'Ah. You need a dinner jacket for an award ceremony. Do you have one?'

'Two. A midnight blue with pale silk lining. It's cute, trendy and slim fit across the chest. And my old dinner jacket. Black. Red lining. Long line. First suit I ever had made to measure. That takes me back.'

'The black suit,' Andy answered before Miles had finished speaking. 'That's the one.'

'Why?'

'Because I am hopelessly sentimental and I know that when you wear that suit it will remind you that you don't have to prove yourself to anyone.

Ever again. You have already been there, many times over.' Then she sniffed. 'And I'm wearing red tonight. Good combo.'

She could almost hear Miles grinning on the other end of the telephone. 'Are you wearing red at this minute?'

Andy glanced down at her less than pristine white strapless bra and Saffie's red French knickers. The red heels were extra slutty and she kicked them off.

'Yes. And no.'

'How much not exactly? Because I am having a vision of red underwear and it is really quite delightful.'

'Is it indeed? Dream on. I am only wearing red French knickers. I mean…I am wearing other clothes but they are not red, and…' She took a breath and sighed out loud. 'And you have the most annoying habit of getting me all flustered. I don't know how you do it. Thank heavens you have already asked me to be your date or I would think that you were trying to chat me up.'

'Red French knickers,' he breathed in a voice of liquid chocolate that warmed her right to the pit of her stomach. 'Oh, Miss Davies. For that I can be dressed and around to your house in about twenty minutes. Get that dressing gown ready.'

'Miles. Stop. Haven't you forgotten something? We have to be on our best behaviour tonight. Remember? My mission shall be to deter other ladies from molesting your fine bod and keeping you company. This is bound to be an arduous task so forget the red underwear. Keep your eyes on the prize.'

'That's what I was doing. Let's make that thirty minutes. I can't wait to see you. Bye for now.'

'Bye.' Her fingers clasped around the phone and closed it, but instead of returning the phone to its charger, she held it to her chest, lay flat on her feather and down duvet and smiled as she waited for her heartbeat to return to something like the normal rate.

Miles Gibson could make her laugh like no other man, and discombobulate her with equal ease. But she dared not tell him. Could not tell him. Letting him know how attracted she was would only lead one way—heartbreak, disaster and unemployment.

One evening. That was their deal. He had kept

his side of the bargain. Now it was time for her to keep hers.

Shame it was so hard to remember that fact when he was so close.

Andy clasped the phone harder.

Why shouldn't she enjoy his company for this evening? He had asked her to be his date. And that was precisely what she was going to be. Because they were friends. Good friends. They trusted one another and they could make this work.

Trust. Yes. She did trust him. Tonight Miles Gibson would be her trusted friend who she could rely on not to let her down.

She smiled and slipped off the bed.

She had thirty minutes to get ready for the best party of her life and, what was more, she had every intention of enjoying it. With Miles by her side every step of the way.

CHAPTER NINE

'HEY girl. Ready to rock and roll?'

Andy stepped forwards into his arms and was enfolded in a fragrant cape of fresh citrus and ice-cool testosterone-infused aroma that was all Miles. He held her close for only a second, his lips pressed into her cheek, before he whispered, 'You were right about the red. You look beautiful. These are for you.'

Andy lifted the posy of red roses and sweet freesias to her nose and inhaled deeply, closing her eyes at the intensity of the perfume.

'Thank you. They are beautiful.'

If it was possible, Miles looked even more handsome than she had imagined. He was dressed in a beautiful hand-tailored black dinner suit that highlighted his broad shoulders and slim hips, and a pristine white dress shirt.

He was so tempting and delicious she could have eaten him with a spoon. And skipped the cream.

Instead she looked from the polished black shoes to perfectly tousled glossy hair and gave a quick sigh of appreciation.

And was thrilled to see his cheeks blush.

'My, you do clean up nicely. Can I add a finishing touch?'

She plucked a perfect red rosebud from the posy and stepped forward so that the front of her black taffeta opera coat was pressed against his chest.

His hands slid behind her back and pulled her closer as she popped the rosebud into the buttonhole of his lapel, slipped the stem into the tiny loop and smoothed down the collar and the front of his jacket with the fingertips of both hands.

'There. Much better.' She smiled and tapped him twice on the chest before trying to step back.

Only Miles had other ideas and held her even tighter around her waist. He tilted his head to one side and ran his smooth cheek up from her jawline to her temple, then her brow, then back to her ear, making her quiver with more than the cold draught that was blowing in through the open door.

'I agree. Much better,' he murmured in a voice that was usually reserved for the bedroom and kissed her so lightly on the lips that she doubted that her lipstick even moved. 'No need to rush.'

He sighed from deep inside and glanced over her shoulder at the staircase. His meaning only too plain. And suddenly the cool draught was not cool enough to calm the thumping heat of Andy's blood.

She swallowed down her overwhelming sense of attraction and pushed it deep inside where she could deal with it later when she was back in her room. Alone.

Take the risk. That was what Miles kept telling her,

Take the risk, Andy. Take the risk and get out there and have the night of your life with this crazy and amazing man who will never know how much you care about him.

She inhaled slowly and turned back to face Miles with a grin on her face.

'I told you that your old suit would be perfect,' she said with a smile in her voice.

'Unlike this shirt,' Miles replied in a choked voice. His chin was high and he had two fingers between the stiff collar of his dress shirt and his throat, trying to create extra space by tugging at the neck. 'Either the collar has shrunk or my neck has got thicker. Possibly both. This is what comes from spending way too much time in offices instead of the beach. Nightmare. I won't last the night at this rate.'

Andy stepped around him and closed her front door, leant closer and whispered into his ear seven clear, crisp words.

'Come upstairs and take your shirt off.'

Miles instantly perked up, his eyes sparkling and only inches away from her face so that she could feel his breath on her cheek. 'I like the way you are thinking but this may not be the best time. Jason will kill me if we don't turn up in the next hour. And what are you doing?'

Andy waved her clutch bag at him, then grabbed his hand and headed for the stairs. 'Like any sensible and organised modern girl, I have a full sewing kit up in my room. I can adjust that top button in a jiffy. Want to follow me?'

'Just lead the way, gorgeous.'

Andy tried to ignore the dark rumblings of innuendo in his voice as Miles positively bounded up the staircase behind her and followed her into her room.

Then stood at the door, frozen and still, as she slipped off her coat.

'Oh, you can come inside. You're quite safe.'

'Shame. But that's not what I am looking at. This is…astonishing.'

'What is?' she asked with a smile and stepped back and turned to follow his gaze.

'I had no idea that you could create something so magical in one room. You've seen Jason's penthouse. Seriously, I had no clue there were so many shades of cream. But this? This is like a rainbow on a dull grey day.'

'It is? I suppose I am so used to it.'

He reached out and grabbed her hand.

'Stand here and try and see what you have created through my eyes.'

Andy took his fingers and Miles stepped back so that his front was pressing against the back of her dress. 'Now. Talk me through each of those posters on the walls. Starting over there.'

He pointed his left arm towards her favourite prints of stained-glass floral scenes and she told him about the great cathedrals she had visited all over London and later Paris with her friend Saffie.

Then the prints of splendid fourteenth-century

Royal manuscripts and Renaissance bibles. The tiny gold icon her father had bought in Greece, of course. And then her own work either side of the window, so that she could see the colours in natural daylight.

And the whole time she had been speaking, Miles had dropped his arms to around her waist, his chin resting on the top of her head, but not just listening for politeness. He really listened. Asked questions. Paid attention.

It was only when she moved forwards to show him her latest drawings that she realised that they had been locked together for over ten minutes!

'Oh, no,' she laughed. 'Look at the time. I am so sorry; I could talk for England once I get started.'

Miles stepped up to the desk and took hold of both of her arms and smiled into her face. 'And I could listen to you talk all evening. Look around you, Andy. You love this. And I should be the one apologising to you. When I saw you in the coffee shop last week, in your little grey suit, I wondered if there was any colour in your life.'

He shook his head, looked around her bedroom and inhaled slowly as he smiled warmly. 'I was wrong. Your joy and your colour are all inside this room. And inside your heart.'

His fingertips pressed against the bare skin of her chest above the line of her dress and she could feel the pulse in his warm skin. 'You have the heart of an artist, Andy Davies. And don't you ever forget that.'

And just like that, her treacherous wounded heart gave a skip and a jump and started singing halleluia.

'Do you really think that I am an artist?' she whispered, swallowing down her fears and pain.

'No. I don't think so. I know so.'

His smile widened into a grin that filled her bedroom with more light and joy than any number of halogen lamps, her feet were an inch off the floor and for the first time in too many long years she felt…happy. And it was such a ridiculous and foolish and girly notion that she pressed her hand to her mouth to smother a giggle.

This, of course, only made him grin more.

'Well, thank you, kind sir,' she smirked, 'but all you had to do was ask and I would have moved your button anyway. Now.' She rubbed her hands together. 'We have a party to go to, so down to business. Sit there on my chair and don't move an inch.'

She reached down and unclipped his bow tie so that it hung around his neck.

Miles watched her in silence as her fingers deftly released the top two buttons on his beautifully tailored silk dress shirt. Undressing him.

'Now don't move or I might jab you,' she warned, and bit down on her lower lip as she bent forwards with her scissors to release the fine stitches holding the button in place.

Her fingertips seemed to have minds of their own and used every opportunity to brush against the fine dark hairs on his chest as she worked. Seconds seemed to take minutes but at last the top button was off and she could sit back and create some air space between them.

His breathing had increased to match hers, and she knew that his gaze hadn't once left her face, which made threading the needle a tad tricky, but she managed it on the third attempt.

By focusing completely on the tiny section of the smooth shirt collar where the button was moving to, Andy managed to hold back from looking into Miles's face. His warm, sensuous chest rose and fell below her hands; his unique scent filled her head with it as she moved her fingers over the lustrous fabric, wishing it were his skin. Each tiny stitch was a triumph of will over temptation so hot and so urgent that if he had grabbed her and thrown her needle and thread out of the window she would have died and gone to heaven.

It was total relief to finally snip off the loop of white thread and create some breathing space between them.

'There you are.' She smiled and busied her hands tidying away the sewing kit. 'I hope it is more comfortable.' She shot one glance at Miles, but he was just sitting there, half turned towards her, watching her with a look that she had never seen before. His hands holding onto the seat, his legs tight together.

Surprise, amusement and what could be admiration or pleasure were all wrapped up inside one single smile.

And something more.

Desire. Hot and spicy and right there, only inches away.

'Thank you,' he breathed in his rich and deliciously smooth voice.

'You are most welcome,' she replied in a strangled voice.

He grinned.

She grinned.

And the world stopped spinning so that they could simply sit grinning at one another. London might be on the other side of the window glass, but at that moment there were only the two of them. United against the world and anything it might throw at them.

Which probably explained why she had no intention of resisting when Miles slid one arm around her waist, tipped her chin up and kissed her on the lips, so tender, so sweet that it took her breath away and brought tears to her eyes.

Her heart was beating so fast she might as well be surfing a huge wave.

'Hey,' she said, with a gentle closed-mouthed smile. 'What was that for?'

Miles pressed two fingers to her warm, moist, soft lips.

'For giving me an insight into a world I knew nothing about,' he replied, and slipped his lips onto the hollow below her ear. 'For trusting me enough to share your dreams.' Andy arched her head back so that his kisses could track down her throat. 'And for turning up to a coffee shop so that I wouldn't be alone.'

He slid back so that he could see her face, and he already missed the way her skin felt, her perfume, the good feeling that came with holding her body in his arms. 'And the fact that you are beautiful and talented and deserve to be pampered on a regular basis. Mustn't forget that one.'

'I am?' she replied in a tiny soft voice, then shrugged and sniffed.

He looked down into Andy's lovely face and saw astonishment and surprise.

And it broke his heart.

After what she had been through in her life, she still had the capacity to care about idiots like him.

The warmth and love in her gaze seemed to radiate into his body through every inch of his skin until they wrapped around his heart and held it tight. Cocooned and safe.

And he melted.

He hadn't intended to. Or expected to. But it happened all the same.

He didn't know what to do with her response. It

was so honest and true and in that moment, in her elegant dress and simple make-up and hair, she looked stunningly beautiful.

And deeply, deeply, desirable.

A deep-seated yearning of naked want started to burn like a raw hot flicker of a flame inside his gut, warming his body in places that he had kept to himself since the accident.

It had been building for days. And working with her in the office had only served to get the coals red-hot and the tinder dry. Just waiting for the spark to ignite them.

Well, here it came.

And instantly he knew. This was a flame that could burn away all of his defences if he let it, leaving him open to all of the pain of rejection.

He should walk away and leave her in this cosy house, with her single bed and her table covered with pens and inks and beautiful designs. Leave her to her safe little world, and well away from the crazy chaos that was his.

Anything else would be too unfair on Andy. He had nothing to offer her but tonight. Long-term relationships were for men who knew who they were and where they wanted to go with their life. Not for men like him.

He rose from the chair, and then clenched his hands into the tiny slim pockets of his dinner-suit trousers, ruining the line and not caring.

'We should be leaving,' he said, only his voice sounded low and way too unconvincing.

She must have thought so, too, because she took a last step and closed the distance between them and pressed the palms of both of her hands flat against the front of his white dinner shirt. He could feel the warmth of her fingertips through the fine fabric as she spread her fingers out in wide arcs and the light perfume enclosed them.

'Don't say any more. I understand. I understand you completely.'

Every muscle in his body tensed as she moved closer and pressed her body against his, one hand reaching in to the small of his back and the other still pressed gently against his shirt. He tried to shift but she shifted with him, her body fitting perfectly against his, her cheek resting on his lapel as though they were dancing to music that only she could hear.

So he did the only thing he could.

He took her left hand from his chest in his right, lifted it high into the air and moved his left arm around her waist and rested it lightly on her hip.

'Did you notice that there will be a dance band at the after-show party? I was hoping you might help me practise a few moves. But with this knee? Don't expect any dips. But could I have the pleasure of this dance, Miss Davies?' he asked in a calm voice.

She stared at him in silence for a second, then slid her right arm from around his waist, flashed him a smile and dived into her clutch bag on the desk next to them and pulled out what looked to Miles like a London bus timetable.

'You are in luck, Mr Gibson. According to my dance card I am free for the next waltz. So yes,' she said, looking into his eyes and holding his gaze. 'You can have the pleasure of this dance. Although I should warn you. The only dancing I do these days is in front of my radio.'

'Forget the waltz.' He smiled and clasped her tighter to his body. 'Did I mention that my mother is Spanish? Dancing is the national sport. I think a box rhumba might work well.'

'I think you are going to have to teach me that one,' she whispered, but her gaze didn't leave his face, her intense focus making his skin and neck burn.

Miles felt her fingers tighten around his arm over his biceps and his heart rate quickened. His hands moved up to her bare upper arms, her smooth soft skin a delight under his touch.

'Back right, side left, forward left, side right. Like a box.'

His left foot slid backwards, taking her with him, back the sideways, their bodies locked together in a rhythm as old as time.

'Listen to the beat,' he coaxed. 'Slow, quick, quick, slow. Hold that slow step. Lean into it just a bit longer. Do you hear it? Do you hear the beat?'

'I think I do,' Andy replied. But her feet stayed where they were as her hands slid up from his arms onto his neck and stayed there.

She lifted her head and her hair brushed his chin as she pressed tentative kisses onto his collarbone and neck. Her mouth was soft and moist and totally, totally captivating.

With each kiss she stepped closer until her hips

beneath her dress were pressed against his and the pressure made him groan.

'Andy,' he muttered, reaching for her shoulders to draw her away. But somehow he was sliding his hands up into her hair instead, holding her head and tilting her face towards him. Then he was kissing her, his tongue in her mouth, her taste surrounding him.

He stroked her tongue with his and traced her lower lip before sucking on it gently. She made a small sound and angled her head to give him more access.

She tasted so sweet, so amazing. So giving.

She gazed at him with eyes filled with concern and regret and sadness as if she was expecting some cutting comment about what a fool she was to invite him to her bedroom—to want to be with him, and only him.

And that look hit him hard.

He did not just want Andy to be his stand-in date for tonight. He wanted to see her again, be with her again. He wanted to know what she looked like when she had just made love. He wanted to find out what gave her pleasure in bed—then make sure that he delivered precisely what the lady ordered.

He went for women who were straightforward. Proud of their gym-and-sports-honed bodies and up front about what they wanted from a relationship. A very short-term relationship.

Which suited him just fine.

Andy was proving him wrong about so many things.

She was as proud and independent as he was. And just as unforgiving with anyone who dared to offer her charity or their pity.

By some fluke, some strange quirk of fate, he had met a woman who truly did understand him more than Lori had ever done. And that was beyond a miracle.

Could he take a chance and show her how special she was? And put his heart on the line at the same time?

He slid a hand down her back to cup her backside, holding her against him as he flexed his hips forward, and one hand still in her hair. She shuddered as he slid his hand in slow circles up from her back to her waist, running his hands up and down her skin, which was like warm silk, so smooth and perfect. He ducked his head and kissed her again, his hands teasing all the while until he was almost holding her upright.

When their lips parted, Andy was panting just as hard as he was. She looked so beautiful, standing there with her dark hair spilling down her shoulders, her cheeks flushed pink and the most stunning smile on her face.

A wave of hair fell forwards as she rested her head on the front of his shirt and he lifted it back from her forehead and tucked it behind one ear before wrapping his arms around her back and holding her tight against him, his chin resting on the top of her hair.

Eyes closed, they stood locked together until he could feel her heart settle down to a steady beat.

All doubt cast aside. Her heart beat for him, as his heart beat for her.

Andy moved in his arms and he looked down into her face as she smiled up at him with, not just her sweet mouth, but with eyes so bright and fun and joyous that his heart sang just to look at them. And it was as though every good thing that he had ever done had come together into one moment in time.

And his heart melted. Just like that.

For a girl who was not wearing much make-up and did not need any.

For a girl who was just about as different from him and his life as it was possible to be.

And for a girl who had made her tiny bedroom the size of Jason's luggage store into a private art gallery and was willing to share her joy with him. And wanted nothing in return but a dance.

God, he loved her for that… Loved her?

Miles stopped, his body frozen and his mind spinning.

He was falling in love with Andy.

Just when he thought that he had finally worked out how to protect himself from being hurt by a woman.

Think! He had to think. He could not allow his emotions to get the better of him.

If he loved her then he should stop right now, because the last thing Andy needed was a one-night stand that would leave her with nothing but more reasons to doubt her judgement.

This was not what he wanted. He wanted temporary. He wanted live for the day.

'I think we might want to rethink the whole

arriving-early-at-the-hotel thing.' She grinned as though she had read his mind.

'Right as always,' he replied, and stroked her cheek with one finger. 'God, you are beautiful. Do you know that?'

Andy blushed from cheek to neck and it was so endearing that he laughed out loud and slid his arms down to her waist and stepped back, even though his body was screaming for him to do something crazy. Like wipe everything off the desk and find out what came next.

He sucked in a breath.

'You are not so bad yourself. I had no idea that sportsmen were such good dancers.' And then she bit down on her lower lip and flashed him a coquettish grin. 'Or did I just get lucky? You are one of a kind, Miles Gibson.'

Lucky? He thought of the long days and nights he had spent training, training, training to the exclusion of everything else in his life, including the girls who had cared about him. Lori had lasted the longest and she'd had her own reasons for putting up with him.

He had sacrificed everything for his sport. *Everything.*

Now as he looked at Andy he thought about what lay ahead and the hard, cold truth of his situation emptied a bucket of ice water over his head.

His hands slid onto her upper arms and locked there. Holding her away from him and the delicious pleasure of her body against his.

'I am not so sure about the lucky bit, Andy. Right now I am struggling to get back into the mad world of the sports business. Months on tour. Constant pressure. And all the while I feel…I feel as though I have lost everything.'

'No, you haven't,' she said. 'You have not lost everything.'

'Don't you get it?' He took hold of her hand and pressed the knuckles to his lips. 'I don't have a career any more. I have been to ten experts and they are all telling me the same thing. Game over. I am finished. Retired. At thirty-one. Have you any idea how terrifying that is? You deserve better than that, Andy. You deserve someone with a dream and a future they can clasp hold of.'

He lowered her hand and started pacing up and down the bedroom, then looked around and suddenly the walls seemed to be closing in on him, and the ceiling was crushing down on him.

It only took him a minute to skip down the staircase, and fumble with the lock on her front door before lurching out onto the small porch, sucking in the air in one long breath after another. Desperate to be outside under a sky. In the open air.

It took him a few minutes to realise that there was a warm body pressed against his back, her breasts tight against his shirt, her arms around his sides.

He grasped hold of her hands and they stood in silence together for so long that the shiver that ran across his back was more due to cold then apprehension of the unknown.

Andy slid her fingers from between his and he turned around and looked at her, his arms at her waist.

And the look in her eyes almost made him lose it.

He was about to apologise, to explain, but she lifted one finger and pressed it to his lips.

'I know two more things about your future career options. No, actually three,' she corrected herself with a blink and a mini shoulder shrug. 'You don't like confined spaces.' And she flicked her head back inside. 'Office work may not be your strength. I am thinking something sports related.' Then she smiled a closed-mouthed smile and rubbed her hands up and down the goose bumps on his arm. 'Warm climate. You are definitely in need of a warm climate.' And then standing on tiptoe she kissed him on the end of his nose, which made him smile despite his best intentions.

'What about number three? Miss career advisor.'

'Hardly,' she laughed, and then ran her tongue over her lips as though she was nervous.

'Just say it,' he whispered, tipping up her chin towards him. 'Tell me what you are thinking.'

She nodded. 'Okay. Here goes.'

She sucked in a breath and ran the collar of his dinner suit between her fingers. 'The Miles Gibson people will see at the award ceremony this evening is strong and worthy of respect and admiration. You have achieved so much and worked so hard to make your dream of being the best surfer in the world come true.' She paused and smoothed down the shirt, her fingers running in long slow tracks.

Then her fingers stopped moving and she looked up into his face as though she was looking for something. 'But that is not the man who wrote those emails and who came to my museum and loves his brother and is willing to take a risk and give me a job so that I can realise my dream. That Miles is capable of reconnecting to his old friends and making new ones and having fun.'

Andy tilted her head to one side. 'Somewhere along the way to being the best and all that work I think you forgot the fun part. And that funny wild and creative Miles can set new goals and get excited about new things and have the best time of his life. That aqua-therapy session was brilliant! You have so many skills and talents it is dazzling.'

Stretching up onto tiptoe, she kissed him on the lips. 'You. Dazzle me.'

She stepped back and patted him twice on the chest. 'You have to say goodbye to the old you and say hello to the new you. Because the new you is amazing. And surprising and inspiring. And he has shown me that I can make my dreams come true in my own way and I don't have to take second best. Ever again. And I will always be grateful to you for that. Always.'

Then she laughed. 'And now it is time to leave before I embarrass myself even more. And I think the car is waiting,' she squeaked, and moved a step backwards with a smile.

He frowned, nodded just once and said something under his breath along the lines of what he did for his brother, then lifted his head, turned towards the door and presented the crook of his arm for her to latch onto. 'Shall we go to the ball, princess? Your carriage awaits.'

CHAPTER TEN

From: Andromeda@ConstellationOfficeServices
To: Saffie@Saffronthechef
Dear fairy godmother. Am emailing from the back of a limo. And I have to tell you—I could get used to this amount of pampering. I have roses. I have a charming prince and your borrowed red shoes are as hard to walk in as glass slippers. Now all I have to watch out for is the clock chiming midnight.
   Totally dreamy. Tell you all about it tomorrow.
   Cinders.

ANDY snuggled back against the sumptuous soft leather seats in the back of the limo and gently spread the silk skirt of her red cocktail dress like a fan on either side of her before patting it with the palm of her hand. 'That's better,' she said to herself.
   Miles snorted out loud, and then gave a couple

of manly coughs into his rolled hand to cover up his laughter.

She play-hit him on the shoulder with her clutch bag.

'Stop it,' she teased, then broke down in her excitement and gave a girly giggle and waggled her bottom from side to side. 'I am having way too much fun.'

Her fingertips fluttered over the smooth fine wood trim. 'I must say that when you pamper a girl, you do it with style. This is definitely a step up from my usual way of getting around.'

'Are you referring to the excellent public transport system in this fine city?' Miles asked while trying to keep his voice calm and serious, but was let down by the telltale crinkling of the left side of his mouth.

She replied by lifting her right leg out high until it almost touched the driver's seat, and twirling her ankle so that the red high-heeled sandal dangled from her toes.

'Regular exercise is essential for the office worker.' She nodded and was about to lower her leg to stop her dress from riding up any higher, but Miles beat her to it.

His warm fingertips clasped around her ankle, his thumbs caressing the back of her foot.

'I'm guessing ballet lessons?'

'Four years,' she whispered from lungs that were too hot to manage a full answer. 'No talent.'

'Worth it. My, you have a lovely ankle, Miss Davies. Good calves too.' He smouldered and ran the palm of his hand the whole length of her leg to the knee, before she grasped hold of those treacherous fingers and lifted them clear of her leg and back to his own.

Only when she was safe of his touch did she lower her leg and tug her skirt down.

'Was that your professional opinion?' she asked in a low casual voice, her gaze firmly fixed on the brightly lit London streets they were gliding down in such quiet and luxurious comfort. Shame that it was in total contrast to the fierce heat burning in her belly from that simple touch of those fingertips on her leg.

'Maybe.' He smiled. 'Maybe not.' And he grinned at her. 'You are looking good, girl. Has to be said.'

Then he turned away, clearly oblivious to the fact that his simple grin filled her heart and her mind with such joy that she wanted to sing and yell and jump up and down on the seat and roll down the window and embarrass herself by shouting out to the whole of London that she was having the best night of her life and Miles Gibson was *her* date!

Her heart was thumping, her throat dry and she was clutching onto her bag for dear life.

Miles was temptation was a capital T.

She wanted to hold his hand and snuggle next to him on the back seat, which was wide enough for some serious semi clad cuddling. *And more.*

Instead she moved one inch closer to the window as they slowed next to the window of a famous London department store. Singing and dancing penguins played on a bright winter scene while Father Christmas flew overhead in his sleigh, packed with gifts, drawn by smiling reindeers.

Miles was going home to Tenerife tomorrow to prepare for a long overseas trip.

And somehow the thought that she would not be seeing him again for weeks, maybe months, was almost too much to think about.

She could send him emails and talk to him on the telephone—if he wanted. *But this was it.* The last evening they would be spending together for a long time. The last time she would be close enough to inhale his fragrance and feel his body close to hers.

He had not promised anything. No long-term commitment. She knew it. *But she could always hope...couldn't she?*

And yet, there was this new idea that kept pushing up. *Live for the moment.* That was what Miles had shown her. *Take the risk Andy. Take the risk, and get out there and have the night of your life with this crazy and amazing man who will never know how much you care about him.*

She inhaled slowly and turned back to face Miles with a grin on her face.

'Don't we make a handsome couple,' she said with a smile in her voice.

His reply was to slide one arm along the back of her seat so that he could tip her chin up and kiss her on the lips, before moving back to grin at her, brimming with self-satisfaction.

'Gorgeous. The press will be far too busy photographing your loveliness to worry about raggedy old me.' He tapped one fingertip on the tip of Andy's nose. 'Dazzler.'

Andy laughed out loud and shook her head.

'Now I know that you have been overdosing on your painkillers. Seriously though,' she added, sitting back, 'is there anyone there tonight who I need to dazzle or watch out for? Because you know that honesty you keep praising?' She sucked in air between her teeth. 'Not always my best feature when I have to be nice to the big cheeses.'

'Relax.' He smiled, and squeezed her hand. 'I do this all the time. The professionals are only interested in the sports personalities and the award winners. There are bound to be a few freelancers who need photos for the gossip pages but they won't bother us. Especially when Lori Wilde is within posing distance. Lori adores this sort of event.'

'Lori Wilde the fashion model?' Andy asked, picking up on the change in his voice and shuffling around so that she could look at him face to face. 'The girl who has that modelling talent show on TV at the moment?'

'The very same. Only when I first met her, Lori was a struggling model waiting for her big break. She was smart, beautiful and ambitious and I talked Jason into using her for our bikini and water-sports ranges. Lori did the rest. We made quite the celebrity couple.'

Couple? Did Miles just say couple?

'Wait a minute. Back up. Are you saying that Lori Wilde was your girlfriend?'

He replied with a relaxed shoulder shrug. 'I thought you knew. We were hard to miss back then. The press loved us. The surfer and the model.'

Miles looked out on the street and nodded slowly. 'We had a spectacular three years. It was Lori who I had left in bed that morning I had the accident. She had a lingerie shoot the next day in New York and I wanted to get some work done before taking her to the airport.'

Three years. Miles had been with one of the most beautiful women in the world for three years!

The bottom fell out of Andy's stomach, leaving a cold emptiness. *What was he doing with her?*

'Three years. That's a long time,' Andy said in a low voice.

'That it is. But we split up after my accident.' He smacked his lips. 'Ironic, isn't it? That I should be meeting her again tonight of all nights.'

'Lori Wilde?' Andy blinked, her brow creased in confusion as her brain struggled to catch up with what he had been saying. 'Lori isn't going to be there tonight, Miles. I went through the guest list this morning with Jason and I would certainly have noticed that name. Are you sure that she was invited?'

'Carlos Ramirez is bringing Lori as his guest. He left me a voicemail message on my personal phone to give me fair warning. Carlos is no fool— he knows that Cory Sports is paying for the award ceremony. He won't do anything to spoil his chances at winning this evening. So don't worry about Lori. She can take care of herself just fine.'

Andy was just about to reply, when the limo slowed, Miles took one glance out of the side window, flashed his signature killer grin and patted her hand.

'Hey, relax. Remember what I said. Just keep smiling, stick by me and you'll be fine. Ready? We're on.'

And before Andy knew what was happening, and could gather her thoughts, the limo pulled slowly to a halt, their driver was at her passenger door and she barely had time to release her seat belt and grab her clutch before Miles took her hand and helped her step out of the car.

To a blaze of flashlights, people screaming and calling his name, over and over again, a crush of bodies and music and colour, which merged into one long blur of overwhelming cacophony.

It was only by physically holding onto Miles as he waved and posed for photographs and forcing her feet to move one step at a time that she survived at all.

As it was, she practically ran through the huge hotel door held open by the liveried doorman.

The red carpet had looked so short when she saw it through the car window, but when she was actually on it? It was a completely different matter.

Leaning deeply against Miles to catch her breath, Andy slumped sideways.

'That. Was. Horrendous,' she gasped between breaths. 'How do you manage to look so relaxed?'

'It's easy.' He smiled. 'You just keep telling yourself that all publicity is good publicity. Cory Sports are paying for this event tonight and the media are going to make money from it. Advertisers, shareholders, everyone in the chain. We need one another.'

Then Miles hugged her closer and whispered in her ear, 'You were amazing. What a star! Thanks.'

'I was a star? Really?' she asked, looking into his grinning face.

A star, he mouthed and pointed at her with a loaded finger. And winked.

And just like that she started to breathe again.

Maybe she could survive this. Even if his gorgeous ex-girlfriend was going to be here. Oh, boy.

One arm around her waist, he turned around and gestured towards a cluster of people gathered at the foot of a long winding staircase. Jason had already seen them and was waggling his fingers at them to come over.

'Shall we go and meet the rest of team? Yes?'

But before Miles could take her hand, a camera crew spotted them and the well-known TV news reporter practically jogged over with his microphone.

'Mr Gibson. Good to see you again, sir. Any chance of a quick interview before the presentation ceremony? I promise you that it will be five minutes at most.'

Miles looked at Andy and shrugged. 'Would you mind? I'll be right here.'

'Not at all,' she replied as though she did this every night of the week. 'Go right ahead.'

Andy stood back and watched him walk away. And within two steps the man she had come to know had gone. Replaced by Miles Gibson, superstar.

She could only stare in amazement as his back and shoulders straightened to fill his dinner jacket to perfection. His chin lifted and he seemed to be taller, slimmer and more elegant than ever before. There was nothing hesitant or undecided in his actions.

Far from it.

His legs strode powerfully forwards to the bank of photographers so that they could get the full benefit of his physique as he gave the interview in a laughing light style, which nobody could ever associate with someone who was in daily pain.

He plunged his left hand inside his trouser pocket, relaxed and in control, and used his right to wave to the incoming celebrities and, in a few cases, to back-slap a passing sportsman and give him a wink and a joke.

This version of Miles was a revelation. Oh, she had seen a glimpse of the media star that first few minutes when he'd marched into the coffee shop that night, but this was something entirely different.

Miles had missed his true calling. He should have been an actor.

He had put on the costume and now he was playing his part as the king of Cory Sports, master of all he surveyed. Proud, confident and totally in control of what the cameras were recording from this event. He turned from side to side, posing and laughing, the consummate professional.

And he loved it. He loved every second of it.

He wanted the adoration of the media—more than that, he seemed invigorated by it. This was what was missing in his life. This was what he had been used to before the accident.

Oh, Miles.

Little wonder that he had probably forgotten that she was still waiting for him.

And it looked as if he could be holding court for quite some time.

Just for a second Andy sighed with regret, then rolled back her shoulders and turned to find Jason. Only to find that he had already moved on to other guests.

Standing next to Jason was a tall, slim and very handsome man who, judging from the applause and the number of photographers calling out his name, was clearly the star of the show, Carlos Ramirez.

And standing only two feet away from her, patiently waiting for Carlos, was Lori Wilde.

Andy had seen her on television a couple of times in her top-rated modelling talent show, where she seemed to be caring and talented, but in the flesh it was disgustingly obvious that she was one of those tall, very slender women who was so naturally beautiful that it was no surprise that the cameras loved her.

Tonight she was wearing a gold Greek goddess column one-shoulder dress, which was so perfect on her it was ridiculous. Her glossy dark hair was artfully arranged into a chignon, softened by trailing wisps at the front.

For a girl that beautiful the only jewellery she needed was a single platinum and diamond collar and matching bracelet. From her ears dangled diamonds that were probably worth the same as Saffie's house.

She could have been posing for a fashion magazine, and Andy froze. Uncertain about what to do, or say, to this perfect creature who had been Miles's girlfriend for three years.

Take a risk, Andy. Take a risk. These things happen. That was then. This is now. Go for it.

And then Carlos was snatched away by a TV crew and the two of them stood there, only feet apart, giving each other furtive glances, while their men were working.

Oh—this was ridiculous. Andy inhaled deeply, smiled and stuck out her hand.

'Hello there—you must be Lori. Lovely to meet you. I'm Andy.'

'And you—Andy. Is that right? I overheard Jason mention your name, but I was teasing him at the time about who Miles was bringing to the event. What a lovely name. Is that short for Andrea?'

Her voice was warm and expressive and lively and such a contrast to the cool and elegant TV persona that Andy laughed out loud. Lori wasn't cold at all.

'Andromeda. Can you believe it? Parents. You leave them unsupervised for a few years and they come up with a name like Andromeda. But I can cope. It suits my classical bent.'

'Oh! Don't get me started about names. Did Miles tell you that Lori is my stage name? He didn't?'

The stunning brunette looked from side to side, then bent down and whispered something in Andy's ear as discreetly as she could.

Andy glanced back to Lori's face. And her mouth fell open.

'No! Your parents would not be so cruel.'

'They would. Even my Scandinavian friends struggle to pronounce my real name. You can see why I changed it. But not a word. It has to be our little secret.'

Andy tapped the side of her nose twice with her forefinger. 'Not a word.'

A huge round of laughter rang out behind them and both Lori and Andy turned around to watch the red-carpet photographers as Carlos played with a football to amuse the crowd. 'Miles tells me that your boyfriend, Carlos, has been shortlisted for an award. You must be delighted.'

Lori's flawless face glowed with genuine delight that no amount of clever make-up could fake.

'Totally. He works so hard for his success. And he's lovely with it. I'm a lucky girl.'

'I would say that he was the lucky one, Lori.'

Lori turned back to her and, without hesitating, gave Andy a one-armed hug, filling the air around her with a sensational aroma of amazing perfume and elegance and class in the second before she released her. 'What a lovely thing to say. Thanks, Andy. We are both lucky.' And then Lori looked up and her easy warm smile shifted to a look of wariness and concern.

Andy was about to reply when a familiar strong arm wrapped around her waist and drew her closer.

'What was that about being lucky? Talking about me again?'

Andy rolled her eyes and tutted. 'Not everything is about you, Miles. I was just saying how lucky we were to be here tonight. It is a lovely party. Isn't that right, Lori?'

'Absolutely.' The brunette stretched out her hand and Miles accepted it as though it were a poisonous viper. 'Nice to see you again, Miles. You are looking well.'

'Same for you,' he replied and took a firmer hold of Andy. 'I hear that you've been spending time in Rio with Carlos. Great city.'

'Oh, you know what it's like, work, work, wor…k.' Lori's gaze slid down to his leg and Andy could feel the muscles tighten in his arm at her waist. 'Sorry, that was insensitive of me.'

Andy smiled up at Miles, expecting him to make some witty and kind remark, but his face was frozen into a look she had never seen before and would rather not see again. White-lipped, tense and with a fierceness about it that brought the temperature of the already cool reception area down another couple of degrees. The air almost crackled with ice until Andy could not stand it any longer and smiled up at Lori.

'Oh, Miles and Jason never seem to stop working. I have only been in their office a few times but the phone never stops ringing and they seem to be dashing about the place all day.'

Lori's eyebrows defied any suggestion of Botox by creasing together and one corner of her mouth twisted up into a half-smile. 'Oh, I'm sorry, Andy. I thought that you were here as Miles's date. I didn't know that you worked for Cory as well.'

'Andy is one of our consultants,' Miles replied for her in a cold, accusing voice. 'But tonight she is here as my date. Isn't that right, Andy?'

And without waiting for her to reply, he wrapped both arms around her back and whirled her up off her feet and into his arms, twirling her twice and making her laugh. Only then did he stop twirling long enough to kiss her on the mouth in a kiss that would have been magical except that the second before his lips touched hers she smiled into his eyes with delight and what she saw there chilled her to the marrow.

His eyes were open. Only they were not looking at her face.

Miles was staring at Lori Wilde and the bank of photographers behind her back, who were only too happy to get some photos of Miles Gibson kissing one girl while his ex and top model Lori Wilde was only a few feet away. Perfect!

And in that instant she knew.

Miles wanted to see Lori's face when he kissed someone else.

Anyone else.

Miles had not asked her to be his date because he liked her and wanted to be with her.

He simply needed someone to be his date so that he could prove to Lori and the sports press that he was over her. More than that—he wanted to rub it in her face that he was capable of finding another girl after his accident.

Or was that dupe an innocent, lonely girl into thinking that he cared about her so that she would walk through that door this evening?

And in that second she made the connection, any happiness and delight Andy had enjoyed that evening were instantly blown away as though they had never happened. Destroyed. Eliminated.

Her happy memory of their evening so far, corrupted and stained.

He was kissing her for the benefit of the cameras and his ego. As far as Miles was concerned she was just an accessory for the evening.

She had been played. Used. *Again.*

Luckily, she did not have to keep up this game of charades for one second longer, because just as Miles lowered her to the floor Jason appeared at his side and whispered something about heading into the main ceremony. Miles instantly released her to look at his watch and talk timings.

Over his shoulder, Andy watched Lori and Carlos walk slowly along the main ground floor corridor, until the backs of their heads were a blur in the bustling crowd of cameramen, TV reporters and elegantly dressed guests.

'Nicely played, Andy. I might not be able to surf but the prettiest girl in London has just made my evening. And that's the truth…Andy? What are you doing now?' He laughed as she shuffled as far away from him as possible and fastened up her opera coat, her clutch bag waggling under her arm.

'What am I doing?' she said through gritted teeth. 'I'm getting my stuff together because I have just realised that I've forgotten something rather important. Is there another way out of the hotel? Apart from that ridiculous red carpet? I need to get out of here right now.'

And without waiting for Miles to reply, Andy strode back towards the main hotel entrance.

'Through the bar, but what do you mean? Way out?' Miles asked, his brow furrowed in concern. 'I thought that you were having a good time?'

'Oh, I was,' she said, her body turning to face him in jerky, stiff movements.

'Then tell me exactly what it is you have for-gotten that is suddenly so important? We are just about to start.'

Andy's fingers balled into fists but when she spoke every word came out burning with fire. 'What have I forgotten? Only this. For a few minutes this week I forgot that I am not prepared to be used by anyone ever again.'

'Used?' Miles looked from side to side and waved at a few of the other guests. 'Andy, lower your voice—you are in the middle of a big public event here. There are cameras. I—'

'No. No. You don't say another word to me. Not now, not ever. You don't get it, do you? You have just admitted it.'

She leant forwards from her waist, her head still, her gaze unblinking. 'You had every intention of using me to make your ex-girlfriend jealous, and make sure that your photograph was on the front page of the gossip magazines tomorrow, and not once—' her voice was shaking now, and she had to take a breath before finishing '—not once did you think about how I would feel. And don't you dare try and deny it, because I won't believe you.'

Closing her eyes through blinding tears she could not fight, Andy forced the words out. 'You didn't invite me out this evening as your friend. You invited me to prove to a lingerie model that you still had some pulling power. Apparently I am just some replaceable girl who you can pick up and put down from the shelf when your ego needs a boost.'

'Andy, no. You don't understand…' Miles moved closer, white-faced, and reached for her arm. But she grabbed her bag and reared away, her feet already heading towards the hotel bar area.

'You are so wrong,' she replied, her voice ice-cold despite the burning in her heart. 'But do you know what hurts the most?' She licked her lips. 'I thought that you were better than that. A lot better.'

And she wrenched her head away and stomped through the crowded cocktail bar, oblivious to the other patrons who were blocking Miles, flung open the side door and was on the pavement before he could catch up.

'Andy. Come back inside. The presentations are about to start.'

Andy slammed the door shut in his face. 'Leave me alone, Miles. I mean it. Because I am not interested in anything you might have to say.'

Her thin-soled red lovely sandals slipped on the wet pavement but she'd turned her back on the man she thought was the centre of her life and strode out into the obscurity and oblivion of crowds of people who thronged the London streets on a Saturday evening.

Miles watched her go for a second, his mind reeling with options.

She was right. So right it shocked him.

He had kissed her for the benefit of Lori and the camera crews, who had lapped it all up. Miles Gibson, stud, was back in town. This was exactly what he had wanted to happen.

But somehow along the way he had managed to fall for the stand-in date. *Big mistake.*

'Andy, wait, please.'

He hobbled down the few steps to the cold pavement as fast as he could, cursing the pain, but to his overwhelming relief her steps slowed before she had gone far.

Andy turned slowly around and looked back at him, her eyes glassy and her face contorted with every kind of emotion that he did not want to see.

She did not speak. She did not need to. It was all there on her face.

'I should have told you about Lori,' he said. 'I

knew that she would be coming here tonight with Carlos. But I didn't know how to handle seeing her again. But that's done now. Please—come back inside.' He waved back towards the hotel where cars were still discharging their VIP guests.

'Oh, no, Miles. I have done that little job you wanted me to do. Haven't I? Just the perfect accessory to make your triumph complete.'

The temperature of the blood in his veins seemed to drop several degrees and a chill spread out from deep inside his belly. Speech was impossible.

Andy moved closer, her gaze locked onto his face, scanning, laser sharp. 'All this week I have been asking myself the same question. Why did Jason set you up on that Internet dating site? You don't need help finding a girlfriend—you never have.'

She stopped, just out of arm's reach, and lifted her head before going on. 'I've just worked it out. You didn't want to meet someone different. Oh, no. All you needed was a girl capable of stringing two words together who could stand by your side on one special occasion. This occasion. That's it, isn't it? You wanted a date for tonight so that you could make sure that your photograph made the headlines. And it took one kiss to make it all crystal clear.'

She moved her head slowly from side to side.

'You're pathetic. Do you know that? Everything you have done and told me during this past week has all been for one reason—to charm me into coming here tonight so that you can prove to the media and that lovely girl in there that you are still the womaniser you were and that she was a fool to break up with you.'

Her chin lifted and when she spoke the words resonated across the cold night air. 'Well, congratulations. Mission accomplished. I hope that you are happy with your work. Sorry I blew it by saying that I worked for you—oh, excuse me. Used to work for you. You should really have given me a script to follow.'

Miles stepped closer, but she backed away as he spoke. 'Andy, give me a chance to explain. Please. Okay, I made a mistake, and I am sorry that you had to find out like that. I should have told you about Lori earlier, but I never wanted you to get hurt. You have to believe that.'

'Believe you? No. I am not listening to another word you have to say. It's over, Miles. Get back inside and do your job. Go. Jason needs you. But Lori doesn't. And that is what really gets you. Isn't it? Lori has moved on and found someone to love while you are still trapped in the past. Tell me I am wrong, Miles.'

She strode forwards, her face rigid with anger, eyes glassy and fixed. 'Tell me I am wrong about Lori.'

'You want to know about Lori. Okay. I'll tell you. Lori didn't just break up with me. She left me. She left me the day I got out of hospital. Because just the sight of my broken, useless body made her feel sick. There. Satisfied now?'

Miles turned away and started pacing up and down the stone pavement. 'The only thing that Lori Wilde felt for me was pity. She felt sorry for me. The minute she saw me in a wheelchair with pins and wires holding my bones together she knew that her fabulous celebrity lifestyle was over. That's why she left. I had stopped being useful to her career any more.'

He glanced back at Andy, who was standing with her arms wrapped around her body, and she looked so vulnerable and fragile he almost slumped down in pain that he had caused her such distress.

'I am sorry, Andy. I am so sorry. This was supposed to be a special evening for you.'

She raised her chin and looked at him with eyes filled with tears, and when she spoke her voice cracked with each word. 'That lovely girl in there cared about you. But you pushed her away. You were the one who told her to go. Weren't you?'

He was thumping his fist into the air. 'After all of those years together she still didn't know me or love me. Lori actually thought that I would be grateful when she offered to stay and take care of me. As if I needed another nurse. I couldn't believe it. So yes, I told her to go and get on with her life and I would get on with mine on my own. And she left. Oh, yes, she couldn't wait to jump on the next plane out.'

'So you drove her away because of your pride. Oh, Miles. Are you still in love with Lori?' Andy's voice was shaking.

'No. Not any more.'

He should have lied. Told her he and Lori were still nuts about each other and she had dumped her current boyfriend the moment she cast eyes on him, walking, talking, polished life and soul of the party just as the old Miles had been before the accident.

But his reply had come out of his mouth without a second of hesitation and as soon as he said the words he knew that they were true.

He had been over Lori for a long time.

Her gaze locked onto his face, with eyes blurred with tears and an expression of the deepest affection and anguish he had ever seen. The emotion in those lovely green eyes rendered him speechless.

'Of course not. There isn't room for anything but your ego. All of this past week I have heard a lot about how you are trying to prove to the sporting world that you are fit and back in the game because you owe it to your family and the business.'

She shook her head slowly from side to side. 'Stop kidding yourself. You are not pushing your body through pain and pretending that everything is okay for the business! You are doing it to prove to yourself that you are still the same man. The champion, the king. Well, congratulations, the press adore you. I only hope it makes you happy.'

Andy stepped forwards so that he could have reached out for her if he'd wanted.

'Everything has come so easily to you, Miles. You have achieved everything you set out to do and more, and instead of celebrating your achievements you put yourself through that little game of charades back there. You have so many remarkable gifts and talents and all you can see is what you cannot do. And do you know what? You didn't just humiliate me just now—*you humiliated yourself.*'

Instinctively he stretched out his arms towards her, but she pushed him away.

'Don't try and contact me. Just. Don't.'

And with that she turned away and he sagged back against the wall and watched the woman he now knew that he was in love with walk away from him. Without looking back. Not knowing that the only person he wanted to adore him was her.

CHAPTER ELEVEN

From: Andromeda@ConstellationIllustrations
To: Saffie@Saffronthechef
Hey busy lady. Hope the Christmas party diners are not driving you too mad. The museum has never been busier with Christmas shoppers fitting in an hour of culture and a coffee break between the stores. Did I tell you that I talked the café owner into stocking that wonderful coffee I had at the Gibsons'? Huge success. I am now high on caffeine and loving it almost as much as my Christmas card sales.

Only two more weeks to go and I can take Christmas off. Bliss.

Madge sends her love. Me too. Andy

'I AM so pleased that you enjoyed the galleries.' Andy smiled into the face of a tiny lady as she popped a splendid book on the porcelain collection into a museum carrier bag. 'But do remember to come back and see us in January,' she added, and nipped out from behind the counter to hand it over in person. 'The new exhibition of ancient Chinese jade promises to be something very special.'

Her last customer of the day gave her a short bow, and Andy was just about to head back to the desk when a stunning and familiar scent wafted towards her from the entrance and she spun around.

And her legs froze to the spot.

'Miles. What…what are you doing here?' she said, her voice thin and high and pathetic as her poor heart tried to cope with the shock of the sight of the tall figure who had strode into the museum shop area. Filling the space with his presence and her mind with exuberant, unexpected and wonderful delight. 'I thought you were in Spain.'

'Hey, girl,' he drawled in that delicious voice that had the power to make her legs turn to jelly. 'I seem to remember that this museum has a great exhibition of illustrated books. Any chance I could have a guided tour?'

'A tour.' She coughed and blinked at his smiling, stunning, amazing face for a few seconds before her brain caught up with his question. 'Oh. I'm sorry. We close in two minutes. You will have to come back…'

But she never got to finish her sentence, because he crossed the few steps that separated them, his gaze fixed on her, wiping out any chance of sensible thought.

Oh, Lord. He looked even more tanned and gorgeous. And smelt better. And every cell in her body screamed out about how much she had longed to see his face. Every day that they had been apart had been a torture.

'I've missed you,' he said with a smile on his lips and in his eyes. 'More than I can say. Any chance that we can get out of here and find somewhere that sells coffee? Because you look good enough to eat.'

Then he walked forwards, pulled her none too gently into his arms, pressed the fingers of one hand into her hair, angled his head and kissed her with every bit of passion and supressed joy that three weeks, two days away from the person you loved could bring. And she kissed him back, matching the touch of his tongue against hers, the hot wetness of his mouth a delicious taster of things to come. She couldn't help it. She had been longing and hoping for this moment to come.

It was Miles who broke the kiss and allowed her to breathe again, and she was just about to go into round two when he grinned and nodded towards the entrance of the museum.

And swung one arm under her legs and the other arm around her back.

Suddenly her legs were swinging in open air.

Because he had picked her up.

And without saying a word, Miles started walking with her kicking in his arms, out of the shop and across the marble paving towards the main door.

Much to the entertainment of the other museum staff and patrons.

Andy squealed out in terror and flung her arms around his neck as she screamed out, 'What are you doing? Put me down right now. I've been comfort eating for the past three weeks. You're going to hurt your leg. Miles!'

His reply was a grin. 'I'm okay. In fact, I am better than okay.'

Andy turned to see her friend the security guard winking at her as he held open the heavy door.

* * *

Two minutes later Andy was standing outside in the still bitterly cold December air with her hand pressed against her mouth, trying not to giggle.

'Well, there goes my reputation at the museum,' she chortled. 'How shocking!'

'I agree,' Miles replied and opened up his long warm down coat so that she could step inside. 'Totally scandalous. Although it does give me some hope.'

'Hope?'

'That maybe I can persuade you to forgive me a little.'

She whisked a stray snowflake from his shoulder. 'Will it involve grovelling?' she asked, trying to stay calm.

'Guaranteed. And this is our ride,' he said and gestured with his head towards the Rolls Royce motor car that was parked in the no-parking zone with the engine running. 'Let's go and get that coffee.'

He opened the passenger door and ran one hand down the length of her arm, and the sensuous pleasure of that simple gesture was too much and in an instant she was snuggling next to him on the back seat of the car.

They sat in comfortable silence for a few seconds, both staring straight ahead, until Andy's heart was ready to burst, and at the exact same time that she turned to ask him what he had been doing Miles opened his mouth and said, 'Did you know it was snowing?'

Then they both burst out laughing and, just like that, Andy felt the wonderful connection between them click back into place, the tension gone in a flash.

'You first.' Andy smiled, and pushed at his shoulder. 'Tell me about the past three weeks.'

'Three weeks, two days, and…' Miles glanced down at a watch that had so many dials on the face it must be hard for him to find the time of day, '…twenty-two hours. Which is far too long.'

Andy inhaled a long slow breath as Miles carried on. 'Taking time out with my folks. Enjoying the sunshine. I made an effort and reconnected with old friends who I hadn't seen for years because of the constant travelling, and competing. And I made a few new ones. And along the way I began to realise something so incredible about myself that had somehow got lost in the shuffle that surrounded the accident.'

His voice had sounded low, calm and confident—but there was just enough of a tremble in those last few words to make her turn to face him.

'What was it? What did you find out, Miles?'

He twisted around on the seat, glanced down and clasped his long cool fingers around hers, before smiling into her face.

'That you were right. That I had lost the simple joy of being with people and family and friends and having a barbecue on the beach and watching the sunset. That I could ask for help and people gave it without asking for anything in return. And that has to make me the biggest idiot in the world.'

Apparently there was something fascinating in her hair, and he released one of her hands to gently pop a stray strand behind her ear as he spoke. 'Yesterday morning I stood on the warm sand on my own two feet and felt the sunshine on my shoulders and I felt happier in that moment than I had felt for years.'

Hair safe, he dropped his hand back to take hers, his eyes on hers. 'And then it hit me. I had to say goodbye to the old Miles, so I could say hello to the new Miles. The Miles who enjoys every second of his life with the people he loves.

Some clever person told me that and I am here to thank her.'

'Do you miss him? The old Miles?'

'No. But I also know I wouldn't have missed being him for the world. Because he helped to create me and gave me a life of glorious Technicolor detail where I was living on the adrenaline rush and sea and surf. And I am grateful to him for that.'

Andy dropped her shoulders and pressed her lips together before speaking. 'The old Miles wouldn't settle for a black-and-white, sepia-tinted life. But what about the new Miles? What does he want?'

His eyebrows rose high but there was a strength in his reply that lifted her spirit.

'I have a new job. Jason and I took some one-to-one time away from the office and came up with a small sports-mentoring initiative. We have used our contacts to pull together a small team of professional sportsmen and women who are willing to share their knowledge with the new young talent coming along. The master classes will be held all around the world but the organisation will be based in London, of all places.'

He frowned and blinked in pretend confusion.

'For some reason Jason thinks that I am the right man to run it. How about that?'

'It's a wonderful idea, Miles. You would be an inspiration to so many people. I know that you helped me. More than I can say.'

'Right back at you. You showed me that business is not just about money, it's about making dreams come true.'

'Me? I showed you that?'

He tapped her lightly on the end of her nose and shrugged. 'Look at you. You made a new life for yourself. And you should be proud of being brave enough to take the chance.'

'Brave? Oh, Miles. Nothing could be further from the truth. For most of my life I have been the worst kind of coward.'

Andy slid her fingers from his so that she could rest her hands on his arms.

'I never told you about my dad, did I? No. You see...'

She looked at Miles, suddenly terrified, but what she saw in his face gave her the courage to carry on. 'When my dad lost his job he had a nervous breakdown. A bad one. He even spent time in hospital.'

She paused, her lips pressed tightly together. 'And when he came out he told me that he felt as though the whole world was pressing down on him, crushing him into the floor, harder and harder until all that was left of him was a greasy smear on the pavement. Can you believe that? A man who used to advise financial directors from some of the world's leading institutions thought that he was nothing but a dirty mark other people walked on?'

She shook her head. 'My parents found out the hard way that when the money ran out and the jobs disappeared overnight, that they had nothing to fall back on. We lost everything. So I started to protect myself from things that had not even happened and my world became smaller and smaller instead of bigger.'

Miles reached out for her hands and wrapped them up, safe and warm, giving her the strength to carry on. 'How did you get through that?' he asked in a low voice full of care.

'I did what I had to do. My parents took off overseas. I was out on my own. So I stopped being curious and adventurous. I couldn't take the risk. I think my spirit was withering and crushed inside of me. Until you came along. And you dragged me out of my comfort zone and forced me to re-evaluate what was important. I thought I knew, but I didn't.'

'Me? I did that?'

'I needed help to face my fear and take control—and start living in the future and not keep making decisions out of fear. And I was scared. I felt as though I were about to cross a great chasm with only one of those flimsy rope bridges attached to each side. I was scared to look down and just the thought of it made me feel sick and dizzy because I knew that if I stumbled and fell, this time there would be no getting back up again. This was it. My last chance.'

She smiled up into the handsome face that was staring at her with such delight and astonishment. And she kissed him on the lips.

'So I shocked Elise and walked away from my job and started work at the museum six days a week. They needed someone to cover the late shift and I was happy to do it. And it means that I have the rest of the day to work on my art and study.'

'Does it make you happy?'

'Yes. It does. *Very happy.* I am never going to

make a lot of money but it is enough and I will create something lovely and special and magical that I will be proud of. You helped me to do that, Miles. Thank you.'

His gaze scanned her face for a few seconds.

'I still haven't forgiven myself for what happened. Lori did care about me—she's a great girl. It was never about her—it was always about me. And I'm sorry that you were dragged into that part of my life. It was unfair.'

One of his hands slid out from between hers and his fingertips glided languorously across her forehead and cheek before lingering on the base of her throat and when he spoke, his voice was soft and intimate. 'That's why I am back in London. I want to see you again, Andy. Very much. I want to be with you. But that all depends on you. Tell me now. Do you think we can get past what happened that night and move on, so that we can be together?'

As his fingertip touched her brow and then her cheek Andy could feel the slight trembling in his touch. He meant it. He truly meant it. And her poor lonely heart forgave him right then and there.

And forgave her treacherous body for not being able to resist him at the same time.

He was looking at her now, a faint hopeful smile on his lips.

'I won't let you down, Andy. Never again.'

'I know,' she whispered and smiled at him, tears running down her cheeks. 'Otherwise I wouldn't be saying yes. Yes, Miles. Yes.' And then she forgot what she was going to say next because he was hugging her so closely and kissing her breathless. Laughing, crying, and then laughing so much that she did not even notice that the car had stopped.

It was Miles who pulled away first.

'Do you see where we are?' he asked with a lilt in his voice.

Andy tore her gaze from his face as Miles opened the car door and stepped outside.

It was the coffee shop where they had first met for the Internet date.

Miles stretched out his hand and, taking her fingers in his, drew her out of the Rolls Royce car and into the coffee shop.

Only it looked nothing like the place she

remembered and she came to a dead stop just inside the door. 'Wow.'

Because there were no customers. No bustle of voices and chatter. Not even baristas.

The harsh white halogens had been switched off, and in their place white pillar candles and candelabra created subtle but warm light.

Spanish music played softly in the background and mountains of fresh flowers in every possible colour combination occupied every corner of the room. Red roses and white freesias spilled out from crystal vases at the centre of each table— but as her eyes acclimatised to the riot of colour and the soft light and shadows her gaze focused on something so familiar she had to stifle a gasp of delight.

The tablecloths had been replaced by white cloths with a single logo—her logo—the one she had designed for Cory Sports, embroidered at the centre in red and blue and gold.

And it looked wonderful.

'Oh, Miles. This is…beautiful,' she whispered.

She looked back, then drew him forwards, clutching his arm as she looked around in disbelief.

'I'm glad you like it. Because this is for you. This is all for you.'

Andy turned around to look into his face. The candlelight caught the snowflakes on his coat and his skin looked golden and warm, as if it had been dusted with gold dust.

'I have an anniversary present for you,' he whispered, and as Andy gazed at him she realised that he was nervous. Which was so new that the final traces of her resentment seemed to melt as fast as the snowflakes. He had done all this for her. And her heart dissolved into mush.

Miles reached into his coat pocket and pulled out a heart-shaped box tied with a wide red ribbon.

'We met for the first time five weeks ago today. And that needs celebrating.'

She smiled to herself and tugged at the bow. A girl could always use more chocolates in her life.

But then she opened the box, and inside was a small velvet jeweller's box nestling in a sea of deep pink fresh rosebuds and white jasmine, the perfume almost overwhelming.

She ran her fingers over the box and the hard

knot of loss she had been carrying for weeks dissolved as she realised what he was doing and why.

Andy swallowed down hard and looked into his face. 'Oh, Miles…'

He stepped forwards and as he spoke his gaze locked onto her eyes and held them transfixed.

'Can you forgive me? What happened at the show was all my fault. I am so sorry for letting you down, and you know that I love you so very, very much.'

'You love me? But I am not one of those sleek girls.'

'I don't want a sleek girl. I want you.'

And then he opened the jewel case and presented it to her. And there, nestling in the midnight-blue velvet, was a pink heart-shaped diamond ring. Brilliant cut, gleaming, every surface reflecting back the candlelight. It was magnificent. And the most beautiful thing she had ever seen in her life.

'I want to give you the most precious thing I possess. My heart and my love. This was the nearest thing that came close.'

Andy looked into his face and her eyes filled with tears.

'You are the woman I want to spend the rest of my life with.' And his voice broke. 'If you will take a chance on a madcap ex-surfer who is looking for love. Real love. Ridiculous, inconvenient, consuming, can't-live-without-each-other love that defies logic and interferes with everything in your life—but you cannot live without it. And I think that love is here. With the girl I am looking at right now.'

He hugged her close inside his coat, then closer, chest to chest, his arms wrapped around her body, his forehead pressing against hers. 'Take a chance on me, Andromeda Davies. Take a chance on the greatest adventure of our lives.'

'You want me? Me? Oh, Miles. Yes, yes, a thousand times yes.'

Miles replied with a great whoop and by grabbing her around the waist and swinging her off her feet and into the air, both of them laughing like children. So happy. *So very, very happy.*

Andy stepped into the space between his legs, looped her arms around his neck.

And it was only as her feet hit the ground that she realised that outside the coffee shop window the snowflakes were falling. Thick large flakes.

The air was thick with them, transforming the London streets into a winter wonderland of white trees and shrubs and statues.

'Miles. Look. Look.'

She snuggled back against his warm, solid chest, which held a heart as wide as the ocean.

It was truly magical. She was in the arms of the man she loved who loved her back in return. And there was nowhere else in this world that she wanted to be.

Because she had his heart and he had hers.

And all because of a few little white lies.

* * * * *

Mills & Boon® Large Print
February 2013

BANISHED TO THE HAREM
Carol Marinelli

NOT JUST THE GREEK'S WIFE
Lucy Monroe

A DELICIOUS DECEPTION
Elizabeth Power

PAINTED THE OTHER WOMAN
Julia James

TAMING THE BROODING CATTLEMAN
Marion Lennox

THE RANCHER'S UNEXPECTED FAMILY
Myrna Mackenzie

NANNY FOR THE MILLIONAIRE'S TWINS
Susan Meier

TRUTH-OR-DATE.COM
Nina Harrington

A GAME OF VOWS
Maisey Yates

A DEVIL IN DISGUISE
Caitlin Crews

REVELATIONS OF THE NIGHT BEFORE
Lynn Raye Harris

Mills & Boon® Large Print
March 2013

A NIGHT OF NO RETURN
Sarah Morgan

A TEMPESTUOUS TEMPTATION
Cathy Williams

BACK IN THE HEADLINES
Sharon Kendrick

A TASTE OF THE UNTAMED
Susan Stephens

THE COUNT'S CHRISTMAS BABY
Rebecca Winters

HIS LARKVILLE CINDERELLA
Melissa McClone

THE NANNY WHO SAVED CHRISTMAS
Michelle Douglas

SNOWED IN AT THE RANCH
Cara Colter

EXQUISITE REVENGE
Abby Green

BENEATH THE VEIL OF PARADISE
Kate Hewitt

SURRENDERING ALL BUT HER HEART
Melanie Milburne

0213 Rom LP